BATTLE
of
BANDS

Sex, Drugs, Rock n Roll & Religion

PAUL MILNES

A catalogue record for this book is available from the National Library of Australia

Publisher:
ASPG (Australian Self Publishing Group)
P.O. Box 159, Calwell, ACT Australia 2905
Email: publishaspg@gmail.com
http://www.inspiringpublishers.com

National Library of Australia Cataloguing-in-Publication entry

Author: Milnes, Paul

Title: **Battle of Bands**/*Paul Milnes*

ISBN: 978-1-925908-39-8 (print)
       978-1-925908-99-2 (eBook)

# The debut novel

This book has been in the making for literally three decades. First putting pencil to paper back in 1991, I wrote the first chapter or so while spending two nights in a hospital bed at Mossman, North Queensland. This was followed by many countless late nights writing bits and pieces over the years, even decades. The past two to three years have been more intense, borderline obsessed with the completion of writing, hiring, and collaborating with professional editors.

The book was born around a handful of songs that had been written and performed. The song 'Carefully Sold' was written on a farm when I was 19 and various other songs over the years.

Having whooping cough in early 2010s damaged my vocal cords, destroyed my confidence, and my self-esteem. Visiting dark and stormy places in my mind, I haven't sung nor played in my band, Lizardskin, or any form since. A feeling of deadman walking cursed me. Writing this story became a positive creative outlet, shining a much-needed light during the darkest of times.

Those who know me well will know I get no better thrill than telling and sharing a good story or yarn over a few beers. I hope you enjoy my first attempt of story-writing and novel.

Sex, Drugs, Rock 'n' Roll, and Religion

This is one lesson I thought I would have learnt from my mistakes. It was the start of a journey riddled of recklessness, booze, drugs, sex, crime, religion, but best of all, rock 'n' roll and good times.

An emotionally powerful story based in the early to mid '80s, *Battle of the Bands* follows the journey of Archie and Lucy Saunders. They leave the familiar comfort of their home on their farm in Victoria, Australia, to start new amongst the hustle and bustle of North Melbourne in a private Catholic school. But the memory of her mother's heart-wrenching death from a tragic horse-riding accident haunts Lucy, and she spirals out of control into the deep, dark, twisted underground in Melbourne, keeping sinister secrets that are hidden behind closed doors. Meanwhile, Archie reaches for the stars to win the Battle of the Bands competition and fulfill his dream of following in his father's footsteps of becoming a singer in a band.

There's only one thing stopping them, an arch-rival band who has the same agenda. 'To win at any cost.' And Lucy's descent into self-destruction.

The Devil's Shoes

It was a warm, clear autumn day in 1982.

The echo of white galahs squawked throughout the terrain. Their wings flapped wildly as our dog, Rusty's, barking spooked the birds. The birds flew to the nearby dry bull oak across our farm, nestling near the border of South Australia and Victoria.

The warm autumn breeze blew through Lucy's long blond hair. Wild sundried thistle along the property sang soulfully while the windmills worked harder than ever.

Mother was dead.

Lucy frequently went down to where Mother's ashes now remained, scattered and spread around the lime tree near the creek, along with Grandma and Grandpa.

Lucy was a happy-go-lucky young girl. She played with her dolls and trucks, sometimes drew and wrote poems. She laughed, cried, and chatted away at Mother's grave near the banks of the slow-running, almost dry Spring Creek, now and then placing flowers she found throughout the property.

Uncle Charlie planted a lime tree when our grandparents passed away ten years ago. They were involved in car accident pulling out of our long driveway at dusk. A slight turn and a ridge created a blind spot. All the locals and farmers would always slow down and were very careful of this section. Tragically, on this occasion, an out-of-towner in a souped-up V8 doing well over 100 miles an hour hit Grandma and Grandpa as they were pulling out and collected them side on.

Dad was touring around Australia playing guitar in a band, doing well for themselves, and had to decide to move back and run the farm, where he eventually met Mum at the local general store.

The creek navigated tranquilly through the valley. It is where Mary, our mother's, life was cut short by tragedy.

Lucy ran back up the hill towards their old Queenslander-style cottage, jumping over dead logs, trying to catch butterflies with her net, skipping, stumbling, and singing made-up songs. Singing to herself, 'Bye-bye, Mummy, Grandma, and Grandpa.'

'Sitting under the lime tree wild, grave is haunting me, scared and frightened like the edge of wood waiting to be used as firewood burnt, then ash, then history.'

'Absorbing and breathing man's mistakes, flowers grow for their own sakes, wastage no more purity,' she hummed away to herself.

Our six-year-old German Shepherd, Rusty, was firmly in tow. We named him Rusty due to his skin and hair looking like the colour of rust when he was a puppy.

✫ ✫ ✫

The day that changed our lives forever...

It was a cold Sunday afternoon on February 10, 1980.

Lucy and Mother were happy and carefree riding on their special white Camarillo horse called Flying Nun, our 12-year-old thoroughbred. They always went horse-riding, especially on a Sunday afternoon after church.

Stable hands nicknamed her Sally after Sally Field, The Flying Nun, due to her sprinting capabilities. After a good career, including six wins and 14 placings in 48 races, Sally amassed a respectable $217,000.00. Dad owned her with a few of his mates. Dad, a horse breeder around the Mallee and Wimmera region, was a jack of all trades. Musician, entertainer, farmer, and wood chopper. The horse had a cult-like following due to her bright white colour.

He had the dream of taking her to race in the Melbourne Cup Carnival, following the footsteps of the legendary trainer Mike Robins and owner Clifford A. Reid with Rain Lover, winning back-to-back Melbourne Cups. The first time was in 1968 by an eight-length margin, also record time. The following year was won by controversy, beating Bart Cummings, favourite horse and a victim of a doping scandal. It was always a buzz going to the track for country races, everyone dressed up, having fun, the atmosphere electric.

In 1979, I was allowed to have 50 cents on Just Dash to win the Melbourne Cup and won. Now and then, Dad would have gigs at the racetrack or the local pubs, sometimes at country music festivals or rodeos. Dad would jump on the bucking bulls or horses from time to time as well. I tried a young bucking horse for the juniors, reaching eight seconds once. Every so often, Lucy would ride as well, but she never lasted the distance, usually being the clown running around protecting the riders. Mum always told her off, saying that it was too dangerous for a young girl. Lucy didn't care; she was a tomboy. She would tell me to go for it and give it all, never be afraid to ask for anything, be yourself, and be courageous.

We would stay in rooms or once in a while camp out under the stars. We had old green sleeping bags. We'd crank up a fire and sit around sharing stories. Best of all, Dad would play us some songs, and we would join in and have a singalong.

Dad gave me a harmonica for my ninth birthday. We sometimes played songs together, mostly blues. My favourite song to play was 'Roadhouse Blues' by The Doors. Lucy's favourite song for the singalong was 'Rocking Robin'. She would always go over the top with the 'tweet, tweet' part, pretending to fly, sing, and dance like a bird.

Mum worked with horses as a stable hand around the Mallee and Wimmera area while doing the odd clerk duties, which consisted of generally being a subordinate directly to the race director or chief steward. Duties included dispatching safety and rescue teams, oversight of track conditions, deploying and withdrawing the safety car, and determining whether to suspend a race in case of dangerous situations. Occasionally, we traveled with her to the tracks as well. Lucy regularly went. I preferred to sleep in. Mum was always up early and would tell us, 'The early bird catches the worm.'

However, on this specific day...

Jonathon Saunders, my father, and I--everyone called him 'Johnny'--were preparing and setting up for one of Dad's gigs that afternoon at the Netherby Pub. It was routine for us. Church, Dad doing a Sunday gig, then back to watch *Countdown* on channel 2 at 6 p.m., a popular pop TV show made by a publicly funded, government-owned national ABC TV network hosted by Molly Meldrum. We loved Molly. I'd never forget when Cold Chisel tore up and smashed the stage live on *Countdown*, smashing the guitars on speakers and amps, Jimmy Barnes holding and sculling vodka. It was awesome. My dream was to play on *Countdown* one day, and tour Australia just like my Dad.

Mum and Lucy rode around the property like any other given Sunday along the steep embarkment of the creek. It was where I went fishing, caught shrimp and yabbies, and looked for geckos, tadpoles or little skink lizards. I remember getting a hook stuck in my finger and Dad having to slice my finger open to remove the hook. That left me in pain for days.

In the saddle, Lucy, tiny enough to squeeze in, sat on the front in tandem, grasping onto Mum's hands, around the bridle and reins.

When they cleared the creek this time, however, Sally pulled up short. When they had to jump the creek like they have done hundreds of times before, the horse tentatively hesitated. Going back over the memory time and again, I was unsure why Sally bucked. She was a lovely horse, no malice in her at all. She may have twinged hurting herself, some form of erosion along the bank, or a feral mad rabbit had spooked her.

Lucy had fallen face first into the shallow-running, clear, cold creek. I could only imagine Lucy crawling back up from the creek bank, showing some signs of hope. Then, horror filled the air.

She climbed up the embankment. An eerie screech and scream echoed through the valley.

Mother gasped, dark, deep, beetroot-red blood squirting from her neck. She had landed on an old, burnt-down, sharp stump, piercing her straight through the side of her throat.

She slowly stood up, stumbled towards Lucy, and held out one hand while the other tried to hold up her neck with the piece of a torn stump. Her eyes flickered. She tried to scream for help. Her voice was scarce, and every time she tried to speak, blood squirted out uncontrollably jet-like, a thin stream gushing from a deep, narrow opening.

She collapsed onto Lucy. Lifeless. Lucy screamed as loud as she could, trembling in the breeze, shaking, holding Mother's head and neck together.

Lucy, Mother still in her arms, was covered in lukewarm blood. It dripped like light rain from her fingertips. The cherry-ripe blood soaked and stained her angelic white dress that Mother had just brought her for her birthday. The arrow shape of the tree stump pierced through the side of Mum's neck like a century-old Japanese samurai sword.

Lucy sat and stared in a state of suffering; as a result, misery quickly flowed into her gentle, kind soul. Warm, salty tears began to flow and shed. Howling like an animal, squealing, screaming, pleading for help, Lucy's screech echoed through the valley. Lucy collapsed onto Mother, begging the Lord to bring her back. Sniffling and weeping, covered in blood, the teary, wet-eyed girl gathered up Sally and rode as fast as she could to the pub. Dad was halfway through the Billy Thorpe's classic 'Most People I Know Think that I'm Crazy' song. Mum and Dad had met at a festival at Sunbury in the early 70s. Dad was a roadie there, keeping in touch with a few musicians. Some would stay over on the farm while touring. Everyone in the pub was singing, drinking, and having a good time.

Lucy barged her way through the crowd. Dad stopped. No music. No sound. I was busy eating the rabbit stew.

'Mum's had an accident. We fell off Sally...her neck.'

The sound of silence made me nauseous.

'Mum's dead, Archie.' She broke down in my arms.

I still remember her small, cold, bloody, and trembling hands on mine. Her eyes, red and teary, were popping out like ping-pong balls. Her white-laced dress was covered in fresh blood.

All I can remember after that was Dad rushing like a bat out of hell to get home.

Dad drove faster and faster, accelerating to nearly 100 miles an hour. The 15-minute drive seemed like an eternity. The old dirty road stretched for a few kilometres before hitting the bitumen. The sound of wind and a flock of black crows took off as we whizzed by.

Storm clouds brewed over the dry, deserted land, quickly approaching as we are destined to drive straight into it. Small drops of rain splattered the windscreen. Dad's screeching old wipers tried to push them away. We hadn't had rain for over six months, with the wheat and barley crops struggling.

It must have been a welcome relief; however, not for us. An unannounced magnificent rainbow appeared amongst the misty rain and clouds. Ironically or coincidentally, it ended near our property.

We finally arrived home.

'Wait here,' Dad demanded. He told us to go inside and call an ambulance.

He raced to the shed and started his dirt bike. Smoke and dust blew out the exhaust pipe, followed by a big bang, that echoed across the land.

Two black ravens took off into the sky. He slid and zoomed past the chicken pen. Hens wildly ran free, flying off to avoid the bike flicking mud in the air as he raced down the valley, mud squirting from the back tyre as he headed towards the creek.

The sound of Father's bike fading in the distance sent shivers through my spine. The rain was now heavy. I could hear Lucy's heart pounding while she sat quivering and crying. Rusty sat next to her, huffing and puffing away, frightened from the sound of thunder and lightning. *Is this a dream?* I thought. The noise of the bike stopped.

There it was, the feeling of the unknown that crept into my body like an unwilling disease. My pulse raced and increased every second. A faint scream of pain bellowed, followed by lightning and massive crack of thunder. Collapsing to my knees on all fours and crawling to my sister's side, I cried and shook like a falling leaf as we held each other, waiting for Dad to return. Even Rusty knew something was wrong. He barked and howled like he was trying to comfort us, while scared of the incoming storm.

The bike started up five minutes later.

We were waiting for the ambulance. The nearest one was about 40 kilometres away back in Nhill. I ran outside to see what was going on. It was getting dark now that the storm had well and truly set in. I could only just see the headlights of Dad's bike through the rain. Without hesitation, I sprinted towards the light.

'Get inside!' Dad yelled as he rode past.

Then I saw Mother's severed head, hanging to her neck by a sinewy thread, dangling and bouncing loosely around due to the terrain of the uphill ride and bumps.

Turning to walk up the hill towards the house, staring in disbelief at the ground. I staggered and stumbled, then violently dry-retched, grasping for air.

Lucy came running down the hill towards me. She stumbled as well, collapsing into my arms. All we could do was weep, sob, sniffling, wiping tears and rain away from our faces. We embraced each other, shedding tears, lamenting, covered in mud, while Dad rode back up to the shed. We couldn't believe it.

Soon, the sirens of the approaching ambulance became more apparent, closer, then louder.

After this, Lucy wore the devil's shoes.

Life in the Bush

It was Sunday morning, and I grew frustrated trying to figure out the Rubik's Cube. Dad was banging vigorously on our door, trying to wake us up.

'Get out of bed, you two. We'll be late for church,' was the cry through the door.

Dad then banged pots and pans together, making one hell of a racket. Lucy and I shared a room. It never bothered me. I mean, I was fifteen months older, but she could be such a spoiled, demanding brat. She always seemed to be up to no good or mischief, an opportunist. I dragged myself out of bed.

'Come on, Lucy, get up,' I said.

Shaking her head, Lucy replied, 'Nick off, Archie, ya wanker.' She rolled to her side.

'Lucy, wake up. Dad will spew at ya.' I gave her another shake.

'I'm sick,' she moaned.

'Yeah, sick in the head, lazy bitch.' I gave her a flick in the back of her ear to encourage her to get up.

Before I knew it, Lucy pounced out of bed quicker than a jaguar, tripping me over and began punching and slapping my head and face. For a twelve-year-old girl, she was swift and healthy, but I was her older brother, and enough was enough. She was about to learn the hard way. Grabbing my Rubik's Cube, she threw it at me, luckily missing my head.

Although unable to figure it out, I liked trying to work it out. It smashed into pieces and shattered all over the room.

'That's it,' I said.

I pushed her as hard as I could against the wardrobe. Lucy collapsed to the ground, moaning. A fleeting feeling of guilt quickly entered my mind. I walked over to check on her.

'Lucy, you okay?' I asked, squinching as I trod on a piece of the broken cube. Bending over for a closer look at my sister on the floor as she gasped in pain, I was taken by surprise again as she clenched onto my hair, pulled herself up, overpowered me, then caught me off guard by kicking me in the groin.

The pain deepened as I struggled to breathe. Lucy pounced upon me, going berserk. She wouldn't stop. Like a barbarian, her punches came out of nowhere, followed by slapping and kicking. I was in serious trouble and needed urgent assistance.

'Help, Dad, help me, please!' I begged Lucy to stop. I couldn't believe I was helpless, being attacked by my younger sister; she was like a mad dog. Dad finally barged into the room, dragging her off me.

Left lying in a pool of pain and blood dripping out of my nose like a leaking tap, I felt weak and dizzy, slightly humiliated.

'What the hell is going on here, you two? You'll end up killing each other!' Dad yelled.

Unable to speak, my mouth moved in silence.

'Arch threw me against the wardrobe,' she said.

'Is this true, Archie?' Dad asked.

All I could manage was to murmur and shake my head.

'Lucy, go eat your breakfast, then get ready for church, now.' Dad pointed in the direction of the kitchen.

Time had passed since our mother's death, and Dad was struggling with us. His drinking became more oppressive; his gigs were not as often as they used to be. We had a bad year with the wheat crop, and his horses weren't quick ones and lost a lot of money on bets. It was all piling up on him. Dad picked me up and placed me on my bed.

'You're badly beaten up, boy. What's going on, Arch?'

I was still in space. My eyes felt like they were rolling faster than a roller coaster; my head felt like a flying saucer zipping around the universe. I wouldn't even try to explain how my groin was. I was a 14-year-old boy. Was I handicapped before I knew what to do with my balls? Would I ever have children? Lucy left me in an inconvenient mess, pain, and aching all over. She was an irritating nuisance.

Slowly and gradually regaining my consciousness and thoughts, I could hear him and see more clearly.

'Yeah, that a boy,' Dad said, still clicking his fingers. 'She laid into you this time, eh?' he said, a wry smile on his face. A rotten stench of stale alcohol smothered my face.

'Time to get you on the punching bag, young man, and show you a few moves and combos, eh?' Dad did a little bit of boxing and martial arts in his teens. He showed us some moves. I wished now he hadn't shown my sister, though.

All I could manage was a sigh, accompanied by a few moans and murmurs.

'Come on, mate. Clean yourself up. Breakfast is ready, your favourite Sunday brekky, bacon and eggs,' he rejoiced and left the room.

He sat there smiling and sipping his coffee. Unable to speak, let alone chew, and eventually collecting my thoughts, I walked into the kitchen. Our radio droned in the background.

'Police charge Lindy Chamberlian, convicted of murdering her baby at Ayres Rock, sentenced to life in prison.' Dad turned it off.

'I never believed that whole story, a dingo took my baby,' he muttered with his mouth full, followed by another hefty swig on his coffee.

Lucy was sitting there eating and smirking at me. I couldn't believe she got away with beating me up. Wiping the blood away that continued to drip from my nose, I wasn't going to stand for this and wanted to seek revenge at the next window of opportunity. Dad had finished his breakfast and went down the hall to the toilet. This was the golden moment I was hoping for. Rusty hung around for scraps. I gave him some bacon, then cautiously surveyed the situation, stalking behind Lucy as she dug into her brekky, unaware of my intentions.

Have you ever been in a situation where you thought it couldn't get worse, but it eventually did?

I reached for the back of her long blond hair and rammed her face into her bacon and eggs. Angrily, I wanted revenge and to inflict some form of pain to my little sister. Oh, what a sight, egg yolk all over her face, with tomato sauce dripping into her eyes! She couldn't see now and frantically started swinging her fists, trying to connect with me. It was too irresistible. I started laughing hysterically.

She wiped the sauce out of her eyes and grabbed her fork. 'You're dead,' she screamed, running like a lunatic, possessed, psychotic, screwball towards me. Her intentions were now visible and noticeable. Her eyes lit up like beacons. This happened all too fast, but I wasn't sticking around to be stabbed or mutilated to death with a kitchen fork by my sister. Lucy went bonkers and chased me around the kitchen, chairs pushed aside, plates crashing to the vinyl floor.

Lucky for me, I was much faster, enabling me to escape. I leapt outside onto the front patio, jumping out of my skin. She scared the living daylights out of me. Our house was like an old Queenslander, so we ran around the big patio, yelling and screaming at each other. I dodged the threatening fork.

'You're dead, Archie!' she yelled as we had a Mexican stand-off. Lucy cornered me.

Dad came charging out, furious, grabbing her arm, snatching the fork, and throwing it over the balcony.

'Calm down,' he demanded. 'Calm down.' His voice came softer while soothing her.

What a morning. We eventually made it to church. We detested going to church regularly, well, usually kicked up a fuss, especially on the way in the car or sometimes on the way back. I remember Dad made us walk back home for a kilometre once, waiting for us at the car with an old cattle yardstick he had, giving us both a hefty swift smack on the bottom. This day was by far the ultimate.

Our father played the keyboard and sang all the choirs and songs, an inspirational leader. I looked up to him as a superhero when he sang. That's what I wanted to do: sing and perform. The looks on people's faces when he sang were amazing.

Lucy and I would sometimes try and sing the hymns as well. Lucy had a really soft, spellbinding voice. It was tranquil, even somewhat at times mesmerizing, whereas mine was more mumbling, mixing the words and making disturbing noises.

Dad explained to me that I was going through puberty, and kids my age's voices always cracked up and croaked before turning into a young man's. It made no sense. I always wanted to be just like Dad, the joy he brought to peoples' lives via his musical talent.

It was a bit harder for him now since Mum was gone. She was the one who kept an eye on Lucy and me while Dad led the church. That day, I got funny looks from people, as I was a bit battered and bruised, as was Lucy.

Everybody who knew us knew Dad would never lay a finger on us, so they knew we'd had another dust-up. Plus, Lucy and I typically attracted some form of attention to ourselves, especially her. She liked the public eye, to be in the limelight. A show pony, I used always to call her. She never cared; she loved ponies and horses.

I remember the snot-nose Jones boy, sitting two rows in front of us, turning his big boof head around, staring at us both, sniffing and picking his nose, giggling at me. His family always sat there. It seemed all the regulars sat in the same spots as we did. I hated that kid. He always looked at us. His red hair, freckly face, pulling faces at me, I couldn't stand him. Lucy slapped him once and chased him with some sticks as well during a heated moment after Sunday school.

To make matters worse, Joanne Cranberry, the first girl I ever kissed, my sweet, first true love, looked at me in disgust, then turned away, shaking her head. Great. Heartbroken, my balls aching, I saw the girl of my dreams turning against me. We had something special and robust going on. We would meet after church school, sometimes behind the old red gum trees. One tree was the nearly the size of a house, and we'd hold hands and have in-depth conversations. We'd talk about the farm and sports. I enjoyed football and cricket; she played netball and tennis. I would always talk about music.

It was the only reason I went to church - to see if Joanne was there. Usually, she discussed the day's mass, to which I just nodded.

We sang in the church choir once a month. I only wanted to do it because Joanna was in it, and I would be next to her. She was an outstanding singer, too.

Our first kiss was behind that tree. It was the most fantastic feeling I ever had, a little sloppy as we exchanged saliva, but I didn't care. She knew everything. She was so smart and beautiful, her long brown hair in a ponytail. She had the prettiest smile I've ever seen and cute dimples. Her beautiful brown eyes: I was transfixed and hypnotized every time I looked into them. Like a daze.

Her mind made my mind like an optical illusion. It was awesome; she always wore a lovely fitting dress to church. She wore a floral cotton dress that day with a wide round neck and small cap sleeves along with a lime-coloured scarf. She looked fantastic. But after being beaten up by my sister, Joanne ignored me. There was no joy today.

My education was limited. We lived so far out of town our, schoolwork was mostly done by radio and isolated. Joanne would also help me out and be my adviser. I honestly did want to learn and be good at school, but most of all, I wanted to be a musician like my dad, a famous rock 'n' roll star touring the world. At the time, my favourite song was 'The Locomotion' by Grand Funk Railway. We played and sang it over and over again at home on the record player. My dream was to record the song and release it.

Dad gave me one of his acoustic guitars for Christmas. I was getting better at guitar and enjoyed playing the harmonica. Dad showed me the chords, giving me heaps of lessons on guitar, along with singing and brought me another harmonica in the key of E.

I was beginning to jam with Dad, which is in the key of A. For whatever reason, you play three chords down or up.

I was never sure. I played by ear and feel. Dad read the music, playing note for note; he would say, 'They're only little notes.'

Music made me feel on top of the world. It was in my veins. To me, music was in our ears and heart; to me, music was life. Better than an education. Dad didn't see it that way. Lucy and I hardly did any schoolwork. We had poor grades. We weren't passing our school via the radio, and that worried Dad.

We constantly got distracted by each other and our surroundings. We would play hide-and-seek as kids around our nearby neighbours' farms. One area has a rock fence, where old Mr. King used to live, his old, burnt-down stone mason buildings, tin sheds, plus rundown cattleyard littered with ancient relics and junk on the property. I would kick the footy around, pretending to play and kicking goals.

I played for the local club, The Nhill Tigers. Lucy played netball as well. She was okay, tall for her age. Her primary position was goal attack. I was small, so played rover changed in the forward pocket. Kicking goals was my favourite, doing snaps and torpedoes. Dad barracked for North Melbourne in the VFL, so I did as well. Malcolm Blight along with the Kraouker brothers, Phil and Jim Krakouer - two of the best indigenous North Melbourne players of all time - were my favourite players. I had number 15 on the back on my duffle coat, after the torpedo goal Blight kicked after the siren to win the 1976 VFL Grand Final against Carlton was amazing. I was young but would never forget how epic it was, being carried off the ground on players' shoulders. Dad had a belly full of beers that day and was going off.

Lucy went for Essendon Bombers. Her hero was local Dimboola legend Tim Watson, plus the flying Dutchman and Daniher brothers. During games, we would collect bottles around the ground.

Occasionally, I was asked to be a boundary umpire for the senior colts; then we would do the scoreboard as well. Payments were nearly two dollars for our work, and if we did a few good laps around the oval, we would make another dollar, collecting five cents from empty cans and bottles for recycling. Lucy was cunning, grabbing drinks still half full and emptying them. That was life in the bush for us.

Announcement

The nearest school was over 40 kilometres away in Nhill, so it didn't surprise me when we were driving back from church when Dad made an announcement, an announcement that I will never forget and that changed Lucy's and my lives dramatically.

'I've been having words with Father McKenzie today, well, for a while now.' Dad turned the radio down. I knew this was serious because we always had the radio loud on the way home.

Our ears sprung up like a couple of little lost mad rabbits when he spoke. You could tell by the tone of his voice something was up.

'He's strongly suggesting,' he paused while wiping some sweat off his forehead, 'that you both need an education and recommends St Joseph's Catholic boarding school.' His eyes squinted and swelled with a tear.

'In Melbourne,' his voice quivered.

My heart stopped. The wind swirling throughout the car was the only sound.

'What do you think about that, guys?' Dad asked, rubbing his hands through his hair nervously.

Lucy and I looked at each other.

'You mean, we go to school?' I asked.

'Yeah, go to school, get an education, and learn something different and real. You two guys don't know it yet, but you're about to have the world at your feet, and I'm afraid I can't teach you everything you'll need to know in the outside world. I mean, my education is limited, you now, and this is a great opportunity.' he said. 'You need to do this for your own sakes. Bright lights, big and colourful people, big business, significant opportunities. So, Archie, what do you reckon? Do you want to go to boarding school in a big city?'

We had never been to a school before, let alone a large city. Just the thought of it made me feel sick and trembling.

'No, not really,' I said nervously.

'Come off it, Arch. It's located near North Melbourne, home of the famous Roos. You can watch a footy game on Arden Street. Seriously, you're 14 years old. What do you want to do with your life when you get older?'

'I don't know, live up here with you, play the guitar.' I shrugged.

Taking a sip of his black coffee, Dad said, 'Archie, if you stay here, you'll learn nothing from the radio school, and I tell you, who is going to listen to your music up here? If you want to live your life scrapping gigs up and playing to the usual suspects locally, then do it. However, I'm your father. I'm suggesting this because it's the right thing to do, and your mother…' He looked towards the heavens, then sighed. '…would also be happy for you to do it? I'm giving you the option to stay here – to become nothing and nobody - or go to boarding school and take music, maths, English, and science lessons at a real school with real teachers; you will live on campus, meet some new people, make some new friends. You know, learn something. Get an education, mate.'

There was a pause in the car as an eagle flew high above, peacefully swooping his prey.

'When?' I asked.

'Next year. Two months, after the summer holidays, the end of January.'

'Do they have music lessons there?'

'Yes, Arch, they do. Plus, you'll both make friends, meet new people, participate in social activities, mix socially with others. Also, see a whole new world open up for you, more than this sleepy old farm.'

'What can I learn?' Lucy scrambled in excitedly.

'Well…' Dad paused. 'You will learn some manners and how to become and turn into a magnificent, beautiful young woman as your mother would wish you to be,' he said with a smile.

'What lessons do I need for that?' she asked, sounding confused.

'Father McKenzie has all the details about all of the lessons that you can take. I can sit down with you both, then you can decide. So, Archie, how does that sound? Do you want to get out of this rat race and move to the big city and go to a boarding school to live?'

'What about you, Dad? What will you do?'

'I'll be okay. I will come and visit you when I can, until you're both settled, confident, and independent on your own. You'll be in the care and faith of the church and the good Lord. They are fathers and brothers at St Joseph's, so you have to behave yourself, unlike this morning's shambles. Okay? None of that!'

I looked at my little sister. She seemed happy and excited for this adventure and opportunity, nodding.

'Okay, Dad, we'll go to boarding school. Melbourne - here we come,' I said.

'Yeah-hoooooooo!' Dad screamed, head out the window, the fresh wind on his face.

That started a trend, so we all began this little ritual. Dad started to make the car kangaroo hop. Lucy unwillingly leaped forwards and backwards.

'Put your seat belts on, kids, and buckle up.' He cranked the radio back on.

We began singing and cheering to 'I Got You' by Split Enz. 'Let's have dinner and get ready to watch *Countdown*, kids!' Dad howled, singing away to the lyrics. 'I don't know why sometimes I get frightened,' he continued, sipping away at his coffee.

So, that was it.

Lucy and I were off to Melbourne as a 14-year-old boy and 12-year-old girl. The school consisted of a primary school and high school for students.

Lucy would begin in year 9, and I would start year 10.

It would be exhilarating for us living away from home without our father and living in different rooms. Lucy and I had become inseparable, especially since the accident.

We fought and argued, but we were more like twins than anything else. We loved each other to death. I was 15 months older than her, although she acted a lot older for her age.

You couldn't compare anybody to her. She was a 12-year-old know-it-all, about to begin her first day of proper school. They pushed her forward a year instead of year 8, and pushed me forward to year 10 instead of year 9, making us both younger than other students in our years.

I guessed she would become independent, in a way, although Dad and the church paid for it all. Then again, I wouldn't trust her if my own life was on the line and depended on it. She witnessed her mother's tragic death, leaving her quiet, angry, shy, and withdrawn. She seemed mentally dull, you know, behind proper time, a ticking time bomb in her own world and fantasy. As a dreamer, she was a crafty, creative, smart, young, and intellectual character. She could act like an angel while wearing the devil's shoes.

Lucy decided her subjects would be art, physical education, music, Australian literature, geography, and drama. They were her choices out of nine, while maths, science, and religion were compulsory. I chose music, advanced English, photography, art, drama, and physical education, while English, maths, science, plus religion, also compulsory.

The time had come. Dad drove us to the Nhill train station. Nearby was the local wheat station, the massive tank with dozens of pigeons nestled in for the day, bird droppings scattered all over the old grey tank. We walked into the station through the vacant porch, stopping and browsing all the old historic landmark photos for the last time on the entrance of the wall, slowly making our way onto the platform under the rusty tin roof.

The Overlander train parked there, confronting; my heart missed a beat. There was a senior woman with a slightly hunched back and one suitcase talking with Father McKenzie, who spotted us; he was six feet tall. I barely recognised him without his usual robes on, only wearing black pants and a black shirt.

He greeted us with a warm handshake, grasping my hand with both of his hands, calmly explaining details and instructions how we would be picked up by one of the brothers at the Melbourne Depot. Looking at Lucy, I thought she was going to crack one of her infamous hissy fits, shaking like a leaf and panting similar to a frenzied paroxysm. I was nervous, but Lucy was a disturbed mess.

The only traveling we had ever done was with Dad for a few of his gigs out of town. This was a six-hour journey, and we weren't coming back. I was packing myself.

'There you go, Arch, that should keep you little whippersnappers out of trouble, so don't spend it all at once,' my father said with his eyes beginning to well, his voice quivering, handing me two $50.00 notes. 'Give one to your sister when you settle in, okay?'

I never had that much money before.

'Thanks, Dad,' I said, feeling a bit on the borderline of joy and emptiness.

Our naked eyes focused. Tolerance and energy had horse-powered through stamina. Dad handed me over a note pad.

'That's to write down your thoughts and new songs ok son'.

Dad took a big breath, winked at me, and said, 'Better get used to that colour of money, boy. I can see it in your hazel eyes. Learn from your lessons, Archie, and learn from your mistakes. If your heart says so, do so. Don't be a dreamer; go out there and fulfill your ambitions and goals and do it. Visualize it and make it happen, okay? Wish for anything you want and work hard to get it. Because if you don't, when you're 66 and look back and wonder where it's all gone...' His voice trembled. '...it'll be too late, mate.' He wiped tears from his eyes, which made me sob like a little boy not being able to go on his favourite ride at a theme park.

'Make a name for yourself, God damn it, and make yourself known,' he continued. 'Never be afraid to ask for anything. Play your guitar and sing from your heart and play until one day it sheds a tear from your eye. Music is my life, but more importantly, my life is making your and Lucy's lives much better and beautiful, okay? There's so much you can do and achieve if you put your mind to it, and with a good education, you will be able to accomplish anything your heart desires.' He gave a hug. 'I'll see you in the charts, Arch.'

'I'll see you in the charts,' he repeated. 'You both have talents and almighty strength. It's all yours.' Dad looked towards the sky. 'Make me and your mother proud, eh?'

We all hugged, sobbed, and laughed. One final goodbye.

'I'll never give up,' Lucy quietly spoke into our dad's ear, her parting words.

I peered down the gravelly, bare train track, the silos in the distance. Rusty came over and rubbed his body over my leg, looking up at me. I leaned down to give him a big cuddle. The smell of dirt, dust, and his usual bad breath panted heavily over my face as I was overcome with emotions from the past couple of months.

Pulling out sundried thistle and bindies out of his tail, it hit me. Becoming severely overwhelmed and breaking down in tears, I cuddled and said goodbye to my dog. He was always happy. It was like leaving my best friend. He was my best friend.

'See ya, little fella,' I said, giving him one last pat on the head.

He licked my face for the last time, panting and puffing away. My dog's brown eyes gazed up at me. He was the best dog ever. It broke my heart and made me tear up again. *I was never going to say goodbye to you, mate.* I ruffled his head again.

The sound of a high-pitched whistle cleared the crisp air from the train.

'The last call to Melbourne. Train departs in one minute,' the driver said while dangling out the door, hanging on with one arm. An eagle hovered above, peaceful and compelling. We repeated our farewells to Dad and thanked Father McKenzie for his generosity, slowly heading straight to the middle of the carriage.

'Remember, guys. Learn and earn, never be afraid to ask for anything, guys, okay? And learn and earn,' our dad repeated as we made our way down the aisle, waving frantically and holding back a whitewash of tears.

I'd never forget that phrase he said: 'Learn and earn.'

'I love you, Dad!' Lucy yelled.

We went to the middle of the carriage, still waving vigorously to our father.

As we started to move, it was bizarre. One minute we had a mum and dad and were living on a farm with our dog without a care in the world. Now we only had each other and 50 bucks a piece. I gazed at the notes before placing them in my wallet.

'Do you think we'll learn and earn anything, Arch?' Lucy asked, snuggling next to me.

We held hands, trying to comfort each other.

'That's up to you now, sis. If you're willing to work hard and put your mind to it like Dad said, we could achieve anything, so yes, you will.'

We watched our father waving goodbye as we looked out the window. Dad blew us a kiss. Our dog barked, then disappeared into the distance while an eagle soared high above us.

'Yes, you will, Luc.' Comforting her, I repeated, 'Yes, you will.'

A senior woman was having trouble placing her luggage in the carriage. I offered her a hand, which she gladly accepted.

'You're the Saunders children, aren't you?'

'Yes, I'm Archie, and that's my little sister, Lucy.' I pointed towards my sister.

'It's rude to point,' the old woman said. 'I knew your grandparents.' Despair coated her frail voice.

'I didn't really know my grandparents. How did you know them?' I asked.

'We used to play golf together, and my late husband and your grandfather were in the war together.'

'Dad told me stories about this, and he had some of his medals hanging up in the music room.'

'Yes, they first met at the Nhill Station Airport barracks. Pilots,' she added.

'Pilots,' I responded, surprised. 'Dad, told me he was a radio guy.'

'Oh, dear.' The lady paused. 'Yes, he did some of that as well.' She sighed.

Talking for an hour or so, I was completely fascinated by her stories.

'I see you around the Netherby Pub, miss, and at the Dawn Services on Anzac Day. You lay a wreath on the monument.' She began to explain how her late husband had passed away and was laid to rest in the nearby Netherby Graveyard, how she popped into the hotel to enjoy and have a couple of beers for him on her way home while listening to our dad perform. 'He has a beautiful voice a great guitarist and wonderful piano player, your dad,' she added with a warm smile. 'I enjoy listening to your father sing, a beautiful voice, a great guitarist, and wonderful piano player,' she repeated, sighing.

I raved on for another twenty minutes or so until realizing the lady was asleep. I went back to join Lucy, who also napped. Her head crunched up against her jumper on the window. Closing my eyes, I was too scared to fall asleep.

Cathedral

'**W**ake up, wake up.'

I vaguely remembered seeing a short, plump, bald man with a light brown and grey short beard, wearing a black robe, slowly tapping Lucy on the cheek.

'Wake up.' His voice became gradually louder.

'Am I still dreaming? Where am I?' I asked.

In a split-second, Lucy screamed, then slapped the man across the side of his face, not once, but twice. We snapped out of dreamland and realized that we arrived at our destination: Melbourne Depot.

The man was Father McKenzie's colleague, Brother John, who was trying to wake us up. Lucy rounded up for another slap; this time, fist tightly clenched. I grabbed her arm to stop this lethal little blow, sincerely apologising to the brother.

'Oh, my God, I beg your pardon. I'm so sorry. Lucy, snap out of it. It's Brother John. We're in Melbourne,' I tried to explain to Lucy, who yawned and rubbed her squirrely eyes.

'Oh, right, sorry,' she said.

The brother leaned over to my ear and whispered, 'Does she normally wake up like this? And please do not use the Lord's name in vain again.' He gave me a wink.

I reminisced about the time she pulverised and beat the life out of me. 'It's been a lot worse, believe me,' I answered.

The brother sighed and shrugged. 'Oh, well, welcome to Melbourne, I guess. My name is Brother John, and you can call me "BJ" for short. Follow me this way. The car is parked up the street a bit. Stay close to me, alright?' he said. 'I'll take you to your new school and home.' He rubbed his hands together. He had a certain swagger about his walk that captivated me.

By now, Lucy full of energy, bounced up, fully awake. We had slept on and off most of the journey. Scrambling to grab our bags, we ambled to the car. We couldn't comprehend or maintain our excitement or believe our eyes or ears. So many cars, so many bright lights, so many people, so many buildings, and such a buzz. It was all happening.

The luminosity of streetlights shining glowed up the whole night. Buildings were more prominent than any trees in our valley. Cars and taxis honked horns.

'Get out of me way!' one driver yelled at a taxi.

It was game on left, right, and centre. A tram the size of a rhino whizzed past us, scaring the hell out of us both. As we drove to our destination, St Joseph's, I was in awe on all the buzz, shimmering lights, people, and noise.

My head stuck out the window like a puppy dog in the bush, the fresh cold wind blowing onto my face and through my hair. Stopping at a set of lights, which I rarely ever saw, the noise of cars and people was overwhelming.

A loosely dressed woman on the corner swinging her hand-bag in circles came to my attention, her hair long and messy. She wore high heels and looked lost. She saw me staring at her. I waved to the woman. She walked directly towards me, her high heels clubbing and echoing through the night's crisp air. Her breasts were huge, the size of the balloons at Lucy's last birthday party. She leaned into the back window where I sat.

'Hi, handsome. Feel like a good time, little man?' Her eyeliner was semi-running, with thick makeup smothered all over her face. Her hair vaguely covered what seemed to be a bruise on the side of her neck. Licking her lips, slowly and gently, she pushed her balloons closer towards me, feeling her hips and legs up and down. She wore a skinny, hot-pink dress. Her terrible body odour wafted through the crisp air, but I didn't care.

'Yes, please,' I replied in anticipation. My eyes lit up. A feeling came across me that had never happened before. I was feeling very excited.

The mystery woman leaned in closer, poking her head into the car.

'Fifty dollars and I'll give you a good time for an hour,' she purred, licking her lips and blowing into my ear. Her voice was deep for a woman. She pushed her balloons towards the open car window and into my face. She carefully examined the car, looking towards Brother John in the front driving.

'All Lucy and I have is 50 dollars between us.'

I hadn't told Lucy about her 50 dollars yet. Lucy bobbed her head into my space, checking out all the commotion. 'Phoaw.' She waved her hand vigorously across her face. 'You smell like some of my brother's stinking jocks.' She slipped back to her side, sniggering.

BJ got the drift of what was happening, scowling at both of us for talking to the strange woman. The lights turned green, and he sped away.

'You do not want to get mixed up with a woman like that, you two. They're foul trouble.'

'What do you mean, BJ? She seemed nice and friendly,' I said.

For whatever reason, there was something about her that delighted me, giving me pleasure and entertainment.

'She's what we call a lady of the night, possibly even a man.'

I stared out the car window again. She was waving at me still.

'Goodbye, handsome. You know where to find me.' Her voice slowly evaporated into the night.

'She sells herself to make money. This street is a junk-fuelled strip, a place where you two young, confused children are not permitted, so no more talking to strangers, okay?' he bellowed.

'Why, BJ?' Lucy asked.

'These streets are riddled with drug users and wars, wheeling and dealing to make money, plus ladies like that are more likely covered with sexual diseases.'

'What are they?' she asked.

'They're what you, young lady, do not ever wish to get and want avoid at any cost when you get older. Remember to stay off these streets, especially at night. You two are way too young to be getting caught up in a crowd and scene like that.'

As the drive went along, BJ explained how things worked at St Joseph's. I observed two guys exchanging items, while another group of guys fought, then descended onto the road, toppling over each other.

'In our school, weekends will be yours, and you can do whatever you like in between activities and Mass. We have a strict, rigorous curfew, but we will shed light on this during your orientation, okay?'

His words went through one ear out the other. I was still thinking of the lady.

'We prefer you to stay close to the campus, and you do need a permit to stay the night elsewhere. Understood?' he barked.

'So, if you're not in bed by curfew, which is 9 p.m., we begin to wonder. There are strict rules to abide by, and we expect you to go by the laws, and of course, most importantly, enjoy your stay and education at St Joseph's. Your dad and Father McKenzie trust our faith and judgment, so please have confidence in us, and the Lord will direct you in your paths.'

Lucy looked like she was in a state of shock; we couldn't believe what we were hearing.

'When we arrive at the campus, you will be straight to bed. It's late; tomorrow is a free day after 10 a.m. Mass, and you will commence school Monday.'

I was still a little excited from meeting that woman while still having that strange feeling like when I thought of Joan Jett or Suzie Quatro.

'What's that?' Lucy pointed to my groin.

I looked down. My penis was more prominent than average. 'I dunno,' I replied, laughing nervously. 'It happened when that woman's balloons pushed up against me.'

We busted out in laughter.

'What's on the radio, Bro?' Lucy rudely asked.

I whacked her on the arm to grab her attention. Wanting to wring her neck for her poor mannerisms, I mean, she just called the brother 'Bro.'

'There was an Australian music show on; I was listening to it on the way here.' He turned the radio back on.

'Beauty!' she yelled. 'Can you turn it up, please, BJ?' She bounced up and down, doing all sorts of weird dance moves. Lucy sat down and buckled up, listening to INXS.

'Can you turn it up more, please? I love INXS,' she said.

So did I. INXS was one the best Aussie bands. I recently read up that their recent album, Swing, the fourth studio album, was the first time they had recorded outside Australia, providing the album's lead single 'Original Sin', peaking at number one for five non-consecutive weeks from early April to mid-May 1984. The album entered the US Top 75 for the first time in the group's history, reaching number 52 on the Billboard Top 200.

I wanted to be in a group like INXS. The lead single 'Original Sin' was the best song, recorded in Big Apple, which is New York City. My aim was to go to the Big Apple someday. I wasn't sure why they called it the Big Apple.

I guess we have the Big Banana, Big Koala, Big Crayfish, and Big Pineapple. Lucy loved Michael Hutchence; she had posters of him and the band on the bedroom wall at home. No doubt she had the posters with her.

My sister always wanted more, more volume, more this, more that, more everything. A beautiful fallen nature. Don't get me wrong. I was no salt of the earth either. Plus, I loved her to death. However, Lucy was a newborn babe, princess of her darkened world, principalities, and powers. She inspired the eternal heavenly angels, sadly in the devil's dress, waiting for that perfect day.

There she sat, swinging, singing, flicking, and humming to herself. Her voice was good, and she could sing. Mum told me 'Lucy' was Latin for 'light' and in church that singing was the sign of heart's joy. Whoever sang well prayed twice over.

Embarrassed, dazed, and confused, vacantly looking out the car window, trying to make sense of my jumbled, disorganised life.

Lucy was singing and leaning towards me.

'Don't change a thing, don't change a thing for me,' she sang, breaking into some weird robot dance and stupid air-guitar head-banging. She thought she could break dance and rap.

Not wanting to muck things up, I had big problems on my hands. If Lucy lost it, I had to be extremely cautious. Witnessing

Mother's death scarred Lucy's eccentric mind. The colour fusion and vision of streetlights flashing, plus the bedlam and pandemonium of people and traffic passing by sent a waft of cold air that shivered down my spine.

'We are nearly there, guys,' BJ said.

Those simple words snapped me out of my daydream and anxiety. Lucy was still jiving to the radio, singing and humming, breaking her moves.

Becoming more high-strung and agitated, I fidgeted and chewed my nails. My new surroundings were local shops, cafes, video stores, takeaway fish 'n' chips, milk bars, liquor and chemist stores, a small plaza, plus a beautiful, big park with pine trees and jaw- dropping manicured small garden beds laced with an array of flowers full in bloom. More shops and a service station were nearby, smothered with old houses and blocks of units. The night glowed down upon us.

Under the streetlight reflection, some graffiti and tags weren't the best. One read *Keep it Real*; another had *T C J. What the hell is T C J?* I was thinking. It was evident this was amateur, no style. There was good red, blue, and orange colours, just no style about it, until we passed an alleyway that had a picture of Bob Marley with the smoke lurking around the brick walls. I loved reggae music; it was also one of my preferred genres. I had his Legend cassette with me, 'Buffalo Soldier', 'No Woman, No Cry', all classics.

Then there it was: a shining cathedral that stood five times taller than our tiny church, bronzed in the evening, full moonlight. My sleepy eyes widened while my jaw dropped. Was this destiny or fate?

Lucy also stopped carrying on and stared motionlessly. BJ turned the volume down.

'This is it, guys. Welcome to St Joseph's.'

There was silence as we drove down the narrow gravel road before we stopped.

'Okay, let's get you two in bed for the night. Follow me,' BJ ordered.

It felt strange creeping around at 1 a.m.

'You'll be staying in my dorm for tonight,' he whispered. 'It's too late to show you both your dorms.'

As we entered his cabin, a soft feeling of warmth and extreme excitement delivered me a pleasing, satisfying smile and experience.

BJ had two single mattresses on the floor with some sheets and rugs.

'There you go. That will do for tonight. You better get some sleep and rest. Breakfast is on at 7 a.m. I will have some delivered by 9 a.m. so you can sleep in a bit. Goodnight,' he said.

We responded, 'Goodnight, BJ.'

'Thanks for everything,' I added while lying down.

Collapsing onto the homemade bed, he gave us a smile and nod, then the lights went out.

We both lay there in the darkness and silence. We were lying there pretty well wide-awake now due to excitement, but still exhausted from the long day.

'Goodnight, Arch,' Lucy said, rolling over and crouching up in a little ball.

'Night, Luc,' I replied, taking a deep breath.

Hearing noises near the window outside, I wondered if it was the boogie man, an animal, or the wind. It sounded like twigs were breaking and rustling noises in the leaves on the ground, gave me the creeps.

Slowly, after an hour or so of tossing and turning, thoughts of that lady crept into my mind, making me feel good again. I eventually drifted off to sleep.

We awoke that morning to BJ tapping a teaspoon on a glass of milk.

'Good morning, guys. Here's your breakfast.' He put a tray on his kitchen table.

The bright morning light shone directly at me, making me squint. I couldn't get out of bed. After pulling the curtains open, he opened the windows and breathed in the fresh air.

'Ah, the sun is out, and it's a beautiful day,' he rejoiced.

We hurried towards the kitchen table and commenced having our breakfast. There was a fresh fruit salad, cereal, and a glass of milk each.

'I have to head into the city this morning and won't be back until this afternoon. Morning service is at 10 a.m. sharp. Lunch at 12:30 to 1 p.m., then the day is all yours. It's up to you guys what you want to do. Remember this, though, this is our place and we make the rules.'

We were reluctantly nodding and agreeing with BJ when a small white, slightly tanned-coloured, Maltese Shih Tzu puppy came running towards us, huffing, puffing and panting away, his soft fluffy furry tail wagging eagerly away.

'Ohhhh, who's this?' Lucy asked, giving the puppy a cuddle and pat.

'This is Chamois, pronounced "Chammy." He's an eight-year-old little boy.'

'He's so soft and beautiful.' Lucy was smitten by the fluffy, little white pooch.

The dog sniffed for food, then ran back, wanting to play. I notice his nuts chopped.

'So cute!' Lucy squealed, throwing a squeaky toy and playing chase and catch with him.

'We have a German Shepherd called Rusty,' I said to BJ.

I missed him already. Snatching the toy from Lucy, it was my time to play.

'Okay, enough now,' BJ said, giving Chammy a cuddle and pulling out a treat from a small jar. 'Let's show you to your rooms,' he explained while sipping his cup of tea.

'Thanks again, BJ,' I said.

'Well, what do you want to do this afternoon?' Lucy asked.

'How about we check out this place, then have a look around the area?' I suggested while making a mess of the breakfast.

'The sun is out. It's a beautiful day to be sitting inside just eating away,' she sang, then laughed.

'Write that down, Lucy. I could use that.'

So, she did willingly.

We decided to walk around the campus for a while, ignoring other students staring at us. We observed an Asian kid being picked on and hassled, a couple of aggressive bigger guys and a girl pushing him, calling him a no-hoper, a chubby Asian, a boat boy, and making the kid cry while they stood around laughing and pointing at him. *It's rude to point,* I thought, remembering what the lady on the train said.

One of the kids punched him in the stomach. The boy groaned, clutching at it. He took off, closely followed by the group.

Lucy went to follow them.

'Come on, sis. Ignore it. Let's go,' I said.

Continuing our walk, we were caught up in how massive the grey-bricked cathedral was, more significant than any red gum tree on our farm.

Inside the entryway, a tall, lanky man wearing a hooded black robe with an Anglican cassock feature overlapping the front, a button closure, and inverted centre pleats addressed us. 'Good morning, children.' He looked directly down upon us.

'Morning,' we replied. I didn't think much of it. He was creepy-looking, and his left eye was bloodshot. He was holding a Bible.

'I am Brother Emmanuel,' he spoke, nodding his head as a welcome gesture.

'Oh, right. Very nice to meet you; thank you so much for your generosity,' I said.

His intimidating presence made me uneasy.

'The action of the Mass takes place in four phases. In the first, we gather together and ready ourselves for all that is to follow — paving the way for the next two parts that form the substance of the celebration.'

Holy smoke, I thought, looking at my sister.

'In the first of these – the Liturgy of the Word – we listen and respond to the Word of God.'

'Um, okay.' I nodded.

He continued, 'Next, in the Liturgy of the Eucharist, we present the gifts, give thanks over them, and receive them back in Communion.'

'Yeah, righto,' Lucy said.

'The fourth and final part – the Concluding Rites – serves to bring the celebration to a close and send us forth.'

'Cool, dude,' Lucy said, peering towards the door.

The man gave Lucy an odd look up and down while giving us an open gesture, directing his arm, then opening the two-part wooden doors. I could feel his bloodshot, eerie eye following us as we cautiously wandered through door, down the red-carpeted aisle. Inside the church were cathedral arcs and high ceilings with stained-glass windows. It took my breath away how beautiful and enormous this place was.

Students scattered, kneeling on timber pews, praying between the arcs and aisles. A young boy walked out of the confession booth with his head down.

I nodded towards Lucy. 'That's where you should go.'

'Bless me, Father, for I have sinned. It's been 12 years since my last confession,' she said, giggling. She pushed me into a pew where another student prayed, knocking him over.

Walking down the central aisle, the medieval-looking organ caught my eye. It was a pipe organ higher than our church put together and nearly as wide as my new dorm built around a solid timber frame. Thoughts of Dad raced through my mind while I stared straight ahead. He mentioned these pipe organs before, how he played one once when he was a teenager in Adelaide. The pipes are divided into ranks, controlled by hand stops, plus a combination of pistons.

Located on the back wall was the Mother of God, the morning light glistening through, shining upon Jesus on the cross. The moment captured me, a spell-binding gift. I was in awe of this place. Our church was an old red-bricked church that would fit about 80 people. This church could hold up to 500 people, at least. We kneeled on the pew, praying for Mother, where she lay in peace, and even for my father. After a couple of minutes, I became emotional. Tears slowly rolled out of my eyes, so I wiped them away and stood up.

'Carn, Luc. Let's get out of here,' I said.

The Gang

Lucy and I decided to head out of the campus, making our way towards the nearby park, talking and absorbing our new neighbourhood. Trams whizzing by us, cars beeping people, all seemed in a hurry. We watched lots of busy people with carts, wheeling and carrying their groceries.

Arriving at the park, we saw there were trees, swings, seesaws, a jungle gym, a sandpit, a slippery dip, a skate ramp, plus a small BMX bike track.

We watched from the seesaw as a group of six kids about the same age as us did all kinds of fancy bike manoeuvres: 180s, jumps, wheelies, and no-handers. We were pretty impressed.

Growing up on a motorbike and bikes, I was right into it, until they spotted us watching and sitting on the seesaw. One kid rode straight up, skidding and flicking dirt and gravel all over us.

'Hey, watch it, you idiot,' Lucy said.

'Oohhhh, we have a real live one here, a real little cute one,' another member joined in, running his fingers through Lucy's long blond hair, twirling it up, and grabbing at the end. 'What's your name, princess?' He leaned in and stroked her cheek, then blew her a kiss.

The group all laughed together. Lucy slapped his hand away from her face. My eyes rolled back, and I rubbed my hand nervously across the side of my face. We were in trouble, and I knew it. Realising now it was the group that had been hassling the Asian boy, Lucy jumped off the seesaw.

I came crunching to the ground hard, slowly knocking the wind out of me, spitting some dust that ended up in my mouth. The plank cracked forcefully into the bottom of this kid's jaw, knocking him backwards off his Redline BMX bike and flying into mid-air. A tooth soared into orbit. The crunch of the impact was shattering, similar to his jaw that was smashed into smithereens. I imagined tiny birds swirling around his head. He no doubt saw stars. He was knocked out cold.

Lucy raced over to a young tree located nearby and pulled out the steel stake supporting it. I couldn't believe this, our first day and she was on the warpath, already leaving this guy knocked out.

Lucy charged back towards the group. 'Who else is going to be a smart arse?' Her face was like she'd been lying in the sun for four hours.

She threatened the group, holding the stake menacingly, swinging and twirling it around like a baseball bat. There was no sound, no movement. They all froze and were taken aback, visibly stunned.

For a twelve-year-old, Lucy was tall and stood out. She aggressively glared at the gang.

'Carn, Lucy, leave it and let's go,' I pleaded.

She looked towards me, snarling like a bull terrier or some other form of a wild, uncontrollable beast. Her face was now purple, ready to burst. She still held the stake, ready and willing to hit a homerun with someone's head.

'Huh, anyone want a go, you gutless pricks?' She stormed over to the guy lying on the ground unconscious, spat on him, and kicked him in the groin. 'Idiot!' she screamed, pacing up and down and around him, continuing to twirl the stake, looking eagerly at the group for anyone to make a move.

The members of the group consisted of two smaller kids who looked older than me, two others about my age, one taller than the other, all wearing jeans, either romes or desert boots, and black T-shirts. While I was positive one of them was a girl about the same age, she wore black shiny pants, black ripple shoes, and a black top, wearing black sunglasses straight out *The Blues Brothers* movie. They were also wearing hats or helmets, so it was hard to tell. They were all staring at me, circling. Expecting the worst, I had second thoughts about staying here. The two smaller ones took off on their bikes.

'Let's go, Lucy. Let's get out the fuck out of here now,' I said.

'You could have blinded us or something you, you dumb ass.' She confronted the taller one.

'You think you're so cool doing your fancy little tricks and stunts on your girl bikes. Who the hell do you think you are?' she asked. 'Well! Who are you? Your buddy here will be like a vampire to me, and I'll pierce him straight through his gutless heart.'

She raised the stake above her head.

Gulping, breathing faster, my heart missed a few beats when a soft-spoken voice from the group said, 'I'm Melissa.'

I knew she was a girl. She was cute, too, reminding me a bit of Joan Jett, with her black pants, black bonds T-shirt, and ripples. Her black hair was similar to the rock 'n' roll goddess as well. She pointed to the guy lying unconscious on the dirt.

'That's my brother Mark you just knocked out. You have probably broken his jaw,' she said, inspecting him carefully, slowly shaking her head, anxious. 'This is Tommy.' She pointed at a guy who looked fit and strong. 'His brother Leigh.' Leigh eyed us up and down. 'And these two knuckleheads are Gazza and Dazza. My brother and I have lived here about five years. Tommy and Leigh were born here, and Gaz and Daz, about three years. They're twins,' she added.

'Yeah, three years,' they both said in sync, joining the group. They were stockier than the others, wearing matching dirty-white bond singlets.

Uneasiness and suspense swirled around in the air. You could cut straight through it with a sharp knife. Stressed, all I could think about was payback.

'Who are you guys?' Melissa asked.

I was instantly attracted to this girl

'I'm Archie Saunders, and that is my lunatic sister, Lucy. I'm sorry about your brother. We arrived last night. We used to live on a farm near the border of S.A. and Victoria, and we just moved here.' I rambled anything to try and suck up to the group, offering her a wry smile.

'Well, you're a long way away from home now, cowboy.'

'We're going to have to fix up our mate now,' Tommy said. 'No doubt we'll see you later.'

The limp body slowly groveled back to his feet while one of them helped him up, placing his arms around them both.

'You okay, Mark?' Leigh asked.

The guy put his hand to his mouth and jaw, steely faced, spitting blood out directly onto my chest.

'Gross, you pig,' Lucy uttered.

It was disgusting and made my stomach turn.

'So, yeah, I guess we'll see you around, eh, cowboy?' Leigh said.

What was with this cowboy business? I wasn't too comfortable with the sound of that at all. I had cold feet and a loss of nerve. She was cute, though retaliation to even the score, I was dreading. They were locals. We were country bumpkins, just two of us. I guessed that was why they called me 'cowboy.'

'Come on, Lucy. Put the stake down and let's go now.'

She threw the stake down, just missing Melissa. She turned around and stopped. I prayed to God this didn't spark up again. Melissa pulled down her sunglass slightly, cocked her eyebrow, then turned away and nestled into the taller guy. Wondering what they were saying, I grabbed Lucy by the arm, dragging her away.

'Now,' I said again.

Her eyes peered at the other girl.

Briskly walking out of the park, bickering and disagreeing about what had just happened and the unforeseen situation we were now in, Lucy remonstrated that they asked for it and started it and she finished it. I had a gut feeling it wasn't over.

'What time is it, Lucy?'

'Damn, my watched has stopped,' she said, shaking her wrist when all she had to do was twist the small knob to restart it.

'I'm hungry; let's go to the plaza and find something to eat.'

We decided on some hot chips at the fish 'n' chips shop. I still had the money Dad gave us. The fish 'n' chips shop was on the corner. On our way, we were still arguing about the incident.

She could be extremely stubborn, and it was so difficult to compromise with her. Myself, I was more a man of peace, a pacifier, no harm on anyone. She persisted, continuing her point of view and case.

'Give it a rest now, Lucy; stop for a moment, will ya? Relax, take a few deep breaths, and count to ten or something.'

'But,' she continued to plead her case.

'But nothing, give it a rest for God's sake.'

When we arrived at the fish 'n' chips shop, my first impression of the plaza and shops was they were ugly and old, full of vandalism, graffiti tags, music posters, and general havoc. One poster stood out, The Court Jester's, a photo of royal coat of arms, and a court jester playing guitar with a smoke hanging out of his mouth. They had abbreviated also to T C J; it clicked that that must have been the tag I saw when we first arrived.

I was cautious and hesitant of walking any further. A man on the ground who looked like he hadn't a shower in weeks was wrapped up in an old stinky rug and placed his hand out, asking us repeatedly for some spare change. Stopping and looking at this man, I saw his hair was grey and tangled, and he was grooming a scruffy beard. He stuck his quivering hand out, motioning towards me. Lucy grabbed me by the arm, pulling me towards the shop.

'What are you doing, man? C'mon on, I'm hungry. Leave the old geezer alone. Remember, Mum always said it is rude to stare.'

'Look at this place, Lucy; it's creepy,' I replied, gazing at the confusion.

'Come on, Arch; you're just a little freaked out right now.'

She ridiculed me, then grabbed my arm, dragging me toward the entrance of the shop.

We made our order and waited. Two men were working, and it was hard to understand them. *Italian or Greek*, I thought. They were arguing and speaking loudly and over the top of each other, waving their hands and arms all around in the air as they spoke. It was gibberish; I couldn't understand anything.

It was funny to watch them, one smaller and the other taller. They acted like brothers or related. I was fascinated by their arms and vibrant, prominent voices becoming louder and louder.

Some kids playing *Space Invaders* and a couple of other video games caught my attention. Playboy and Kiss pinball machines were there; we had a quick game of that while we waited, giggling and sniggering at the moaning and groaning sounds coming from the Playboy pinny.

'Number 89, your chips are ready.'

I gave the man a quick thank-you nod, walking out of the shop feeling a little amused and relaxed.

We began slowly eating, waiting until our food cooled down. We burned our mouths and fingers a little as we walked back to the campus four blocks away. They were lovely chips, the best hot chips I'd ever had: chicken salt, vinegar, and a drizzle of tomato sauce. The best way to 'ave 'em.

As we were walking, stuffing our faces, and blowing on the hot chips, a volcanic noise erupted nearby, something like out of *Bathurst*. A Florentine-gold, metallic GTS Monaro Holden with two broad 'go-faster' stripes down the centre and twin air scoops in the bonnet rumbled passed us, the engines like jet planes. It had black vinyl seats and fainted, tinted windows.

'Wow, check that out,' I said to Lucy.

She was more interested in the chips.

'That is special, reminds me of Uncle Charlie's car. An old factory-original 1970 HG GTS Monaro 253 V8 and four-speed Saginaw gearbox.'

I had some knowledge about cars from when we used to visit my uncle. He had car magazines and took us to car-swap meets where he lived on a small property near Millicent, located on the southwest coast of South Australia.

Suddenly, a voice appeared.

'Hey, you little missy!' shouted someone from the back seat, over the top of David Bowie's song 'Modern Love'. The car engine revved, and a massive noise from the exhaust ripped through the empty streets.

Sweat slowly rolling from my forehead, my heart beat loud and fast. Lucy was more concerned about the roof of her mouth burning from the mouthful of hot chips.

'Ignore them, Lucy; don't say a word, please,' I begged. 'Just keep walking.'

'Where's your stick now, you sick little bitch?' Tommy yelled, pulling out small knife and waving it in our direction.

'Well, what do we do now?' Lucy asked through a mouthful of chips.

'Nothing. Just shut up and let's make a run for it.'

The brakes screeched. On that note, we made a run for it back to the campus as fast as we could. Voices raged. What a predicament, we had a massive dilemma on our hands.

They began to drive off again, following us and screaming abuse and honking their horns, trying the hardest to run us over. Butterflies began to suffocate my panic-stricken body.

'You're mincemeat, princess!' one yelled, flicking his cigarette towards her.

'Keep going, Luc!' I tried to catch my breath.

The intersection drew closer. The streetlight motioned, flicked to amber.

Bugger this, I thought.

'Quick, Lucy, we'll make it.'

There was an intersection, dodging cars, sounds of wheels and brakes screeching on the hot black bitumen road.

'Watch out, dickhead!' a passenger yelled.

I avoided traffic as best as I could, like the game of *Frogger*.

Shiiiiit, we're in trouble now.

I turned back in fear, hoping to see my little sister. Car engines revved, accelerating, and horns honked me. Brakes screeched. I was packing myself.

I watched Lucy gritting her tongue between her teeth and running frantically across the intersection; her hot chips went everywhere. As the cars took off, she began to dodge, weave, and even jump over a vehicle to the chime of horns and cars crashing into each other. Lucy finally made it across the road.

'Watch it, you crazy little bitch,' was the cry from the driver who Lucy jumped over like a flying jezebel.

I looked back towards the Holden, and it was held up due to the red light and three cars back.

'All right,' I celebrated to myself. 'Let's go, Luc. Quick, this way.'

We continued to run back to the school two blocks down and lost them. We slowly sneaked back into school. We hid and did not want them to know where we were staying. It was just after 3.30 p.m. when we made it back to BJ's room. Pacing around the room, I tried to regroup and catch my breath. I felt like strangling her. Alarms were going off in my head. She really caused some trouble this time. I was petrified, wanting to go home, and missing my dog terribly. I hated this place. I punched the wall, leaving a small fist mark on it.

Spontaneously, we looked at each other, her blameless and shameless eyes shadowed by her blond fringe. She erupted in laughter.

'Did you see the face of that guy in the car I jumped over? That was a classic,' she boasted.

I was annoyed, and we began to argue again. We argued until I was sick and tired of being sick and tired. No sense occurred out of it anymore. Lucy kept to her side of the story, then she finally stopped. Not listening or biting back anymore, she gave up while only talking to herself. Walking over to the sink to get a drink of water, I heard an unwrapping sound. I turned around to see Lucy munching happily on a chocolate bar.

'Where in the hell did you get that?'

'I bought it,' she replied.

'I have the money, Lucy.' My voice rose in anger yet again.

'I found a dollar in the seat of the train when you were talking to the lady.'

'Why? Do you want a bite?' she asked, smirking, thoroughly enjoying the bar.

I didn't know whether to believe her, considering we had lost the chips during the heat of the chase. I was hungry and accepted her offer, as dinner was hours away, and I had to eat something. That was a close shave, too close for my liking.

First Day of School

It was time for the first day of school.

Monday couldn't come around quick enough. The last 48 hours seemed too surreal.

First came the introduction Principal Jones. Dressed as a priest, he was tall and slim, in his fifties, with a distinctive limp. He handed us our books and school uniforms: grey pants and a white collared shirt, blazer and dark blue jumper, plus a dark blue tie for me. Lucy's was a dark blue checkered outfit and jumper. You could tell by her screwed-up nose she didn't like it. The man thoroughly explained the rules and his expectations.

He told us to join the other students at the cafeteria for breakfast, as we were running late. Arriving at the café, we were the last ones. There were not many people left, so we quickly decided to have some porridge and juice. By this stage, we were both excited about our first day of school and dressing up in our uniform. Well, I was anyway.

BJ escorted us to our sections of the school, showing us around. Lucy went to her school area to her first class while

I was off to my domain to my first class, which was advanced English, followed by music.

'Hello, Archie, I am Miss Reeves,' she said.

'G'day,' I replied, noticing there was only one table and chair remaining. I gathered it was mine.

The teacher introduced me to my classmates, and I was greeted with murmurs, grunts, giggles, and the odd hello. Becoming unsettled, my mind drifted off as all the events from the past 48 hours filled my thoughts. I investigated and scoped out the room. Miss Reeves was asking various students to spell words and explain their meaning.

To my surprise, my name was called out. 'Archie,' the teacher kept repeating until I awoke out of my daydream.

'Yes?' I answered.

'Spell "spontaneous" and tell the class what it means,' she said.

My heart missed a beat, and my eyes rolled over. Hopelessly failing to spell the word and having no idea what it meant, the result was the class laughing as they gave me odd looks and pointed fingers. This was a feeling that I have never experienced before. I had never been in a classroom, let alone being singled out.

A girl in front of me spelled it out and explained it meant a happening or arising without an apparent external cause. She turned back to me, giving me wry smirk.

'Well done.' The teacher applauded.

I wanted to sink into a hole, then was saved by the bell. As the siren sounded, all the students packed their books, filled their pencil cases, and left for the next lesson.

The teacher asked me to stay behind for a minute, as nearly every kid peered at me on the way out. 'Archie, come here, please,' she politely said.

'Yes, ma'am,' I replied, making my way to her desk.

'Listen, I know you've never been to school before and that you used to study at home and by the radio,' she confessed. 'Welcome to the school. Take your time adjusting, make some new friends,' she suggested. She spoke with a calmness in her voice.

'I think I already made some,' I muttered. My eyes darted all over the place, unable to look her in the eye.

'Excuse me? What did you say?'

'Ah, yeah, righto,' I replied, even more anxious.

'Archie, look at me in the eyes when I'm talking to you.'

Her tone instantly put me on my back foot, so I quickly looked up at her as she requested. Her long face frowned down on me, making me feel uneasy. I looked away again.

'I write songs, poems, and good stories. I got A's last year for my stories,' I eagerly explained, even though schooled via radio. My eyes were still unable to look at her. I instantly didn't like her. She pushed me to look her in the eyes while talking to her. I was becoming more frustrated.

'A's,' she mimicked.

'Yes,' I answered.

'Well, time will tell. For your homework, I want you to write a 500-word story.'

Whatever, I thought, nodding.

'Look me in the eyes when I am speaking to you,' the teacher demanded.

I agreed reluctantly, briefly glimpsing at her eyes again.

Relieved that was over, I raced off to my next lesson, which was what I had been waiting for: music. I had been looking forward to this for weeks. I was late for the class after getting lost and arriving in the wrong classroom. At last, I walked into the right room.

My heart missed a beat as the teacher introduced herself.

'Hello, Archie, I am Mrs. Boothby,' she said as I noticed a few members of the gang we had an altercation with. Tommy was glaring at me while Melissa was sitting next to him, shaking her head, rolling her fingers through her hair, and muttering to herself. First impression, she looked beautiful.

'Class, this is Archie Saunders. He has joined St Joseph's today, so please make him welcome,' Mrs. Boothby requested. She then directed me to my seat located at the back of the room and away from the other two.

I sat down. Melissa and Tommy looked towards me while he suggested with his finger as to slice my throat. I could lip read what he said: 'You're dead.'

Terrific, I thought, *this is just how I should have expected this to be. The only people I know or have met Lucy has threatened and beaten one. Now they want to get back at us or me, and they're in the same school.* It was safe to say by this stage that I wanted to go home.

The lesson began with some theory and more theory, which I knew nothing about. I played music by ear and read the chords. Dad could play note from the notes. I never really bothered to notice them.

The teacher began talking. 'The most frequently encountered chords are triads, so called because they consist of three distinct notes: the root note and intervals of a third and a fifth above the root note. Other chords with more than three notes include added tone chords, extended tones, and tone clusters, which are used in contemporary classical music and jazz and different genres.'

What the hell? I thought, trying to catch a cheeky glimpse of Melissa.

The teacher was playing composers from the 1700s and 1800s: Bach, Tchaikovsky, and Beethoven.

Who are these people? Apart from Beethoven, I never heard of them. The music sounded nice. I Hadn't heard of this kind of music before.

The teacher put me on the spot and asked me what kind of genre this music was. I didn't even know what genre meant. I couldn't answer, and again, the class began giggling, peering, pointing, and talking amongst each other.

'Um, I'm sorry, ma'am. I don't really know. I do like it, but I have never heard of this kind of music.'

'Who can tell Archie what kind of music this is?' the teacher asked the class.

We didn't have these records back home. I was bamboozled.

'Awkward,' Melissa mumbled to herself, putting up her hand.

The teacher acknowledged her. 'Yes, Melissa?'

'It is classical.'

'Excellent, well done,' the teacher said.

I put my head down in shame and began reading again; this theory was confusing.

'Triads consist of three notes, the root or first note, the third, and the fifth,' she continued. 'For example, the C-major scales consist of the notes C D E F G A B. A triad can be constructed on any note of such a major scale, and all are minor or major except the triad on the seventh or leading tone, which is a diminished chord. A triad formed using the note C itself consists of C, the root note, E, the third note of the scale, and G, the fifth note of the scale.'

Whoa, slow down. My brain was in overload as I looked blankly outside the window.

'The interval from C to E is of four semitones, a major chord, and so this triad is called C-major. A triad formed upon the same scale but with D as the root note. D, root, F, third, A, fifth, on the other hand, has only three semitones between the root and third and is called D-minor, a minor triad,' the teacher explained.

What the hell? My brain was spinning, then luckily the siren went again.

The kids packed all their belongings and hurried off to recess. On the way, Tommy and Melissa glared at me.

I walked down the corridor, my head down in shame, when before I knew it, Tommy grabbed me and threw me up against the locker.

'Hey, cowboy,' he said before punching me straight in the stomach.

I lost my breath. He quickly hit me again, directly in my eye. I collapsed. He kicked me in my ribs, and I struggled to breathe. Someone stormed down the aisle.

'Break it up, break it up!' It was a man's voice.

Thankfully, it was BJ.

Tommy and his mate ran off, disappearing amongst the crowd.

'Who did this to you, Archie?' BJ asked.

All I could manage was a few groans. 'I'm not sure,' I replied. It was my first instinct to not tell. 'I was hit from behind.'

'Who saw this?' he yelled at the onlookers.

No one said anything.

'Come with me.' Picking me up, he took me straight to medical for treatment.

Meanwhile, Lucy was also in a similar position with her new surroundings, lessons, and classes. She had even crossed paths with Gazza and Dazza, the twins in her second lesson as well. During recess, she had a half-boiled egg thrown at her face, leaving her with a fat lip; someone had burnt her hair with a lighter. Funnily enough, we both met in the medical area. Some of the flames also singed her neck, and she required ice on her lip.

'That's it, Archie. This means war.' Smoke steamed out of her ears.

'Lucy, give it up, will ya? If you never acted as you did in the park, this would never have happened.'

'Bullshit,' she snapped. 'That guy started it by flicking dirt on us and provoking us in the park.'

I knew she was right, but I seriously wanted this to stop and blow over but couldn't see it happening.

'I'm going to build a kero bomb and throw it in their room while they're asleep tonight.'

'No way, Lucy.'

We used to make those on the farm and throw onto hay bales and watch them go up in smoke. 'Just give it a rest, okay?'

About 20 minutes later, we were released, and the day went on just as badly as it started. More questions to answer that I didn't know, more stares, and of course, more classes with Tommy and Melissa, while her brother Mark was still in hospital sporting a broken jaw.

The last lesson of the day was photography. I saw Melissa, who came over to me.

'I hear you didn't tell Brother John or Principal Jones that Tommy did it,' she said.

'Yeah, well, if I did, I gathered this would only get worse, so I thought it would be easier to hopefully only have one beating and get on with it.'

She smiled; she was pretty. I could see my reflection in her beautiful green eyes. I couldn't believe how I felt when she was around. My first day had finished and could not have come around sooner.

I met up with Lucy so we could get ready to go for dinner together. We entered the room, and it was full and seemed like all eyes were on us, me sporting a fresh swollen black eye, and Lucy with a fat lip.

'Come on,' I said. 'Let's just get our dinner and leave.'

'I'm grabbing a steak knife for later,' Lucy replied.

'No, you're not.' I shook my head, dragging her to the line to wait for our dinner.

It wasn't too bad. Grilled chicken, mash, and veggies were on my plate while Lucy went for the T-bone steak, chips, and salad.

While I was enjoying my dinner, someone tapped my shoulder. I looked over, and someone blew pepper straight into my eyes. It stung like hell, and I was unable see. Reaching for a handful of potato mash, I threw it at the culprit. A handful of pasta hit my face. Standing up quickly and blinded by the pepper in my eyes,

I thought, *Is this how the rabbits felt when I used to catch them on the farm, laying bricks near their holes, placing pepper on it?* They would come out and sniff up the pepper and knock themselves out on the brick. I would sell them for fifty cents each to the local pub, and they would make rabbit stew for Sunday special.

Not funny now, is it? I was thinking. I stumbled over chairs, getting pushed and whacked with more food. An unknown person shook up a can of soft drink and sprayed it straight at my groin and face.

Bee-lining straight toward the exit, the 90-plus packed cafeteria cheered on what seemed to be an all-in food fight now. The chef followed me and tackled me to the ground.

'You're not going anywhere, mate. You started this, so you're cleaning it up.'

Picking me up by the collar and dragging me back in towards the kitchen, he poured cold water in my eyes. I could finally see. The place eventually cleared out, leaving a few other students and me with the mess to clean up. I was filthy, dirty, and now angry at the situation I was in. BJ had walked in the cafeteria, asking how I was settling in.

'Great, thanks, BJ,' I said on my hands and knees cleaning mash and vegies off the cold vinyl floor.

Lucy was nowhere to be seen. I noticed various blood spots splattered over the floor and some chairs. I frantically cleaned the stains up while BJ talked to the chef, both looking towards me during their conversation. *What the heck?* Rolling my eyes back, I was on the lookout for my sister. This was our first day of school.

Hours

I went to meet Lucy and clarify some news with her. I had been trying to call Father for days, but the phone has kept going to the message bank. We hadn't heard from him this week. The last letter we had was over two weeks ago. As we walked towards our dorm, two guys were harassing and bullying the same Asian kid we witnessed before. The kid was clearly beside himself with being victimised, weeping, and begging for them to stop.

'Oi!' I screamed.

The two guys threw him to the ground and ran off. I was sure one was Mark, who had slowly recovered from his injured jaw. It wasn't broken, just smashed up a bit, but he did lose a tooth. The altercation was about fifty metres away, so I wasn't sure who the other guy was. As I began to walk toward the kid, he dragged himself off the ground and ran off.

'Yeah, no worries, mate!' I yelled as he scrambled for safety.

'Why bother?' I mumbled to myself.

Walking off, I spotted the brother that I had seen at the church entrance the other day, peering from where I assumed were his sleeping quarters. Dressed in the usual dark robe, his hood covered most of his face. He saw what happened and did diddly squat, just wore that weird, eerie smirk. Turning around, he walked back into the dorm with the small puppy dog in tow, wagging his tail.

There was something about him that made me feel uneasy. While walking away, I heard the door close. A young female student walked out briskly, looking around and fixing her hair while running off. It was weird, but so was this man.

Catching up to Lucy, I filled her in while she also kept me updated on her week. We were very excited due to the weekend, she informed me that we had finally received another letter from Dad. Lucy read it to me while I sat there gawking out the window.

'Hi, guys,' the letter read. 'Hope you're both well and behaving. Please make sure you listen to your teachers and Father McKenzie. Archie, I hope your music is going fine.' This brought a smile to my face. 'Make sure you do all your homework. The farm has had a little rain.'

Lucy kept reading out loud. My smile soon turned into a frown as I smelt and noticed a steak knife on her study table and a soft drink bottle half-filled with liquid and a rag.

'Ah, Lucy, what the hell is all of this?' I picked up the items designed for destruction.

'Ummm, I found them,' she replied hastily and continued to read the letter.

'You're not blowing up that guy's room, and I hate to think what you have in mind with this steak knife.'

I grabbed the items and stormed out of her room towards the garbage and placed the gear in the bins. I spotted the kid who had been getting harassed sitting by himself and wiping his eyes. I went over to him and asked him if he was okay. He looked up at me. I knew Mark was the perpetrator. This kid was younger than me, slightly overweight with thin line of blood trickling out of his nose.

'You alright, mate?' I asked, walking towards him cautiously.

'Those- those boys always pick on me, call me names, take my ma- ma- money, throw away my lunch, and broke my f- f- flute,' he said with a stutter and a twitch.

'Your flute? What assholes.'

'I'm sick of it.' He wept. 'They'll get theirs one day.'

'What's your name?' I asked, trying to comfort him.

'Hieu,' he answered.

'Hi? Yes, okay. Hi, how are you? So, yeah, what's your name, mate?' I asked again, a little confused.

'My name is Hieu, pronounced "Hi," spelled H-I-E-U.'

'Ah, okay, no worries, mate. That was a tricky one. Well, it's good to meet you.'

'Don't worry about it for now, okay?'

We chatted for a while. He told me his parents were boat people working hard for ten years, saved up their money, and started their own property development business. They work 14–15-hour days, six days a week, which was why they sent him to the school. The idle chit-chat continued for a little longer, until I asked about his stutter and twitching.

He explained that he had Tourette's, which was a common neurodevelopmental disorder he got when he was a child. I had never heard or saw anyone with Tourette's before.

Tourette's Syndrome, TS, or simply Tourette's is characterised by multiple motor tics and at least one vocal one, a nervous system disorder involving repetitive movements or unwanted sound, such as repeatedly blinking the eyes, shrugging shoulders, or blurting out offensive words.

Hieu told me that treatment included medication and many psychological therapies. I had never met anyone like him before. I took a quick liking to him and formed a mutual respect and bond with this kid over time. We would hang out and share stories. He was a unique, fascinating person. I found him to be an extremely intelligent person who always talked about computers, numbers, and maths while I bored him with music, girls, and sport.

We were all in the high school band. Hieu was on his flute, and I played clarinet. We became good friends due to the fact we played the only wind instruments in the band. Daz on bass, Gazza on drums, Melissa on piano while Tommy mixed it around with violin and guitar. We had to play a Johan Strauss composition, 'The Blue Danube Waltz'.

I learnt a lot about the composer in music lessons, that he was born in Vienna, I really wanted to go there some day. We had to learn Wolfgang Amadeus Mozart's work and Vivaldi's 'The Four Seasons' for a school concert once.

Lucy was singing and training in classical music, and all of us were in the church choir. Our music teacher made us study several musicians, including Bach and Ludwig Van Beethoven, Mozart's junior by 15 years, Beethoven was immensely inspired and influenced by Mozart's work, with which he became acquainted as a teenager. We learnt that Beethoven eventually travelled to Vienna with the aim to someday study with the older composer.

Our teacher explained to us that some of Beethoven's work resembled Mozart's and was very comparable, like his composition cadenzas, and Mozart's D-minor piano concerto. For a country boy, I was quickly swept up in it all.

I was in deep thought when Hieu spoke softly. 'Them boys and girls will pay.' He stuttered, then yelled, 'Karma's a bitch!' He looked towards Tommy and Mark.

'Them boys and girls will pay. Karma's a bitch, mate,' he stuttered and muttered under his breath again. 'There will be blood.'

It was impossible, yet all true, but these teenagers put their own twist on their destinies. I could tell all he wanted was payback and that someday he would. I thought he was just angry, so didn't take much notice until one day, a day that changed the lives of all us at school.

I headed towards the cafe for tea to meet Lucy as per usual. Sure enough, Mark had sights for Hieu. The poor kid had had enough and brought his father's .22-caliber gun into school. He ran into the vicinity where Mark and Tommy had been playing handball against the brick wall and pointed the gun straight at Mark. Hieu pulled the trigger, firing directly into his chest. Mark violently crashed into the wall.

Tommy split like a jezebel around the corner and out of sight. Hieu casually walked up to a lifeless Mark lying on the ground in a pool of claret and pointed the gun towards Mark's head.

'You always pick on me, Mark, no more, no more!' he yelled.

He shot him again, fair square, directly in his face. Marks' brains and parts of his mutilated skull splattered across the wall and asphalt. Hieu opened fire, sending crackpot shots towards anyone and anybody in range, frantically twitching while doing so.

The cracking sound of gunfire echoed throughout the school, students scattering for their lives, while he shot towards another group of kids. I froze, standing about 30 metres from him. He pointed the gun in my direction, his hands shaking. The sun glistened brightly on the barrel, his eyes red, teary, and blinking.

'No, Hieu!' I screamed. Exposed, I placed my hands out in front of me and tried to protect myself. 'Put the gun down.' I gestured towards the ground.

'Please don't,' I begged, eyeballing straight down the barrel of his weapon, petrified.

Light rays reflected from the sun off the tip of the barrel, near blinding me. He took a deep breath, blinking, twitching. His eyes were swollen, fresh tears running down his cheek. He took a deep breath.

'Your good man, Archie, a good man,' he said, stuttering. In the blink of an eye, he put the gun under his chin.

I ran towards him, tripping and falling over my own feet. Tommy flew around the corner and crash-tackled him to the ground.

Bang! Gunfire went off, another thunderous roar throughout the campus. An eerie silence. They both lay there, motionless, seeming an eternity.

'Tommy!' I screamed, scrambling, stumbling towards him.

He was sprawled out on the asphalt, groaning and grasping his shoulder.

'Are you okay?' I asked.

'Have I been shot?' He panicked, checking his body for bullet holes. He tried to stand, only to fall back onto me.

I caught him. 'Fuck knows, man. I dunno, dude.'

'Argh, my shoulder.' Blood poured from the wound.

Hieu's gunshot grazed his shoulder amongst the crash-tackle.

'You slanty-eyed freak!' Tommy yelled, booting Hieu fair square in the face, not once, not twice, but three vicious times.

I grabbed Tommy to stop him. Strong as an ox, he shrugged me off. BJ came running towards us, demanding that he stop. Looking around and observing the carnage, I saw the crimes against humanity standing in a puddle of blood.

Mark was unrecognisable, brains spattered across the brick wall where we played handball. Hieu's massacre killed Mark and seriously injured others. The sound of sirens and the police soon arrived. The school was in lockdown, cordoned off as investigators examined the area. Not long after, ambulances arrived, more police followed with a news crew. Chaos erupted. Police held them back. Cameras pointed everywhere. Students scattered and observed from a safer spot. One officer seemed younger and staring at me, breathing heavier behind a wall of doubt.

A slightly sophisticated female reporter holding a microphone was trying to get information out of anyone and everyone. She asked me questions that didn't resonate with me. It was a blur being in a state of shock. The cameraman jostled into position amongst the blood and carnage.

'Breaking news,' she began. 'We are live.'

The woman cleared her throat. 'Police have charged a teenager with murder concerning a massacre here in North Melbourne's St Joseph's private boarding school. They found a man with a gunshot wound to the chest and face, who died at the scene.' The woman began to tweak at her ear, adjusting her earpiece. She paused and seemed to answer a question.

'Yes, that's right, another student has been shot in the back, who is yet to be formally identified. Four more are seriously injured with gunshot wounds taken to Royal Melbourne Hospital.' Another pause as she held her ear, trying to avoid the pools of blood scattered across the ground, her high heels catching some.

'It's bloodshed here, Steve. Police say they believed the shooter and the victims knew each other, and they did not believe there was any further threat to the community,' the reporter continued.

Melissa appeared from the café, walking towards us in shock and demanding to know what happened to her brother.

A policewoman dragged her away from the catastrophe. Watching on in disbelief, I could see and hear Melissa screaming hysterically, tears streaming down her face, trembling then collapsing onto the ground, traumatised. It was an eerie feeling and impossible to avoid. I wanted to accompany and protect her, but I was helpless. Even dark stormy clouds have a silver lining.

Hieu was taken into custody, then charged for murder. He was tried as an adult for murder. The families and friends of those killed and injured said they wanted the death penalty to be reinstated and demanded he was never released from prison. If convicted of capital murder in court, he could be eligible for parole after 40 years. Little comfort to the families.

We never heard from that boy again. His fate was committing suicide, strangling himself inside his cell, leaving a disturbing goodbye letter for his parents, labeling it '4 Hours', explaining why he did what he did. It was fair to say not much bullying or harassing students took place that year while our worlds had been turned upside down, giving us all unsettling dreams. A stillness so dense, deafening the ears of the group, desperate and indecision followed how God works in mysterious ways.

'4 Hours'

There is a passion inside of me
An infatuation kind of disease
I told some friends, and they all laughed at me
So, tell me what else could I do
When I went to sleep that night
I didn't want to go to school
The girls, they picked on me
The boys treated me like a fool
So, tell me, what else should I do
Yeah, and I'm serving my time
The servants and sermons have been declined
So, this is why I write this song to you
Yeah, I've only 4 hours left in my day
So, Momma and Poppa, please forgive me
Those boys and girls, they all picked on me
So, this is why I write this song for you
God, help me, what else could I do
Yeah, and I'm serving my time
The servants and sermons have been declined
So, this is why I write this song to you
Yeah, I've only 4 hours left in my day
I remember that day at school
Yeah, when that boy, he picked that fight Before I went to sleep that night
I found my poppa's gun
And that boy became target number one.

Audition

Time had passed. It took a while for the storm to move between the gang and us, then one day after school, I went back to the music room to pick up the music book that was left behind. I had recently written some poems and songs and was eager to go over them. While I approached the room, a classic version of a Rolling Stones cover, 'Sympathy for the Devil', played. I stopped and really listened to the voice. It was pretty tight, although the vocals where a bit off and flat. Waiting until the song finished, I poked my head in to have a peek and hesitantly walked in. The gang was all gathered there.

'What the hell do you want, cowboy?' Tommy yelled.

'Just getting my books, man.' *What's with this cowboy shit? I thought. Sounds good, actually.* Out of nowhere, I blurted, 'I think the vocals need a little more reverb... that's all.'

Leigh was there at the sound desk, touching and turning knobs. He eyeballed me over, staring angrily. I must have hit a nerve or something.

'Just saying from where I am, you know, just a little tweak.' I gestured.

'Try that, Gazza,' Leigh said.

Disgruntled, Gazza nodded in approval.

'Are you guys forming a band or something?' I asked inquisitively.

'Piss off, Saunders!' Gazza yelled over the microphone, hiding behind a massive drum kit. He must have been the vocals, as he was the only one with a mic. To their surprise, it did sound a lot better.

'So, you're the one trying to sing?' I smiled cheekily.

'Just leave, Saunders,' Daz said, flicking some cool bass riff.

Grabbing my books and notepad, wishing I had eyes in the back of my head, I walked down the hallway. Deciding to turn around due to my paranoia, an ad on the notice board caught my eye.

'Singer wanted. Auditions this Friday after school for "Battle of Bands" competition,' the ad read.

That was it; I knew straight away.

Photography was the last lesson of the day, so this allowed me to speak to Melissa about it. Itching out of my skin, the time had come. Highly strung, I returned to the music room and approached Melissa. Everyone else had left.

'Hey, Melissa, you guys sounded really cool this morning.'

She gave me her usual wry smile and turned back to doing what she was doing, ignoring me.

'I'm serious. You sounded excellent. I play the guitar as well, plus harmonica. I can also sing. My father is a musician. He plays the piano and sings at our local church back home and plays guitar. He toured Australia. Well, now he plays gigs locally.'

She turned to me. 'Listen, Archie, my brother Mark was...' She paused as her eyes welled up. Gathering herself back together, she continued, 'Mark was our singer, okay? But your sick, twisted sister smashed his jaw, which made us miss a Battle of Bands competition. That's why Tommy gave you a beating, and now, well, Mark is dead.'

'I'm sorry, Mel. I didn't mean to.'

Mel cut in, 'We want to form a band to compete for the Battle of Bands. First prize is $1000 cash and an 8-hour recording session. So, we need a singer really bad. I mean, Gaz is alright, and Tommy is okay, but Mark, Mark was an unbelievable singer.'

She reminisced, thinking about her brother. 'Mark had an awesome stage presence about him, like no other.'

'I can do it,' I pleaded. 'I also write songs; here, look! I wrote this one, called it "Carefully Sold". I passed her my note pad showing her the lyrics.

Reading the song, she glanced and gave a smile that would have made Stevie Wonder happy.

'Mmmm, this is pretty catchy actually,' she said. 'Although there's no way on earth Tommy and the boys will allow this to happen.'

After another pause, I could see my reflection in her green eyes. I smiled at her.

'Have you written any more songs like this?' she asked.

'Yes, yes, many. Even Lucy writes poetry.'

Her smile made me feel lukewarm and fuzzy all over again.

'Um, well, I dunno,' she mumbled.

'Come on. What we got to lose, Mel?'

'Ah, fuck it, the audition's tomorrow tonight after school. Good luck, cowboy, you will need it. Also, keep your hot-headed sister away, alright?'

I practiced and practiced in my room for hours. When it was time for the auditions, the day seemed to start out as usual, but then dragged on for what felt like an eternity. I showed up for the auditions with a skip in my step.

'Get the hell out of here, Saunders. You're not welcome!' Tommy yelled.

There were only four other students to audition, so I knew I had a one-in-five chance.

'I was hoping you could give him a go,' Melissa said. She was eager to hear me and to move on from the silly battle between us.

The four others had their audition; knowing that I was better than any of them, I was the last person for the spot.

'No way, Saunders; piss off,' Tommy yelled again.

'Come of it, Allan Moffat. Give us a break, will ya, Tommy?' I said. 'I never dobbed on you when you gave me the flogging a while back, and the shit with Hieu, man, give us a crack.'

Bugger it. I grabbed my acoustic guitar out of the case, plugged the lead in, and ignored Leigh's attempt to stop me, then commenced to play the Rolling Stones song I had heard them play. I began the first verse, strumming a few chords, E, D, and A. Melissa followed with some sweet-sounding keyboard. Daz on bass also joined in while his twin brother, Gazza, slowly kept up on drums. Tommy stood there looking on. As I sang, Tommy reluctantly joined in.

Come the first chorus, we were all pretty much on song. By mid-way through, it just felt right; the chemistry of the song, the timing, the musicianship, it all fell into place.

I pointed to Leigh to turn up our front speaker. As he did this, Tommy and I could hear that we were in harmony, not trying to compete. I pulled out my harmonica and let rip with a howling harp solo. Tommy and I started jamming the blues together. It was an angry blues battle, but an enjoyable one. He was ripping out solo and lead break that Keith Richards would have given the thumbs-up to.

We finished up and all seemed pretty happy, apart from Tommy. Confident that I was better than the rest of the students who had auditioned, I could tell by the others that it was a great jam.

'What do you think?' I asked the group, my head held high and full of confidence.

'We'll have a band meeting and let everyone who auditioned know by Monday,' Tommy said.

I grabbed my guitar, thanked them all, and waited until Monday. I exited the room, feeling reasonably confident and more importantly, happy with myself. Melissa gave me what seemed a nod of approval. I would give a million bucks to go out with her. She was so damn cute.

Overwhelmed and generally anxious about the news to see if I made the cut to be in the band, I could think of nothing else. It was driving me crazy. I was getting ready, enjoying a packet of Chicken Chickadees, washing it down a Tarino orange soft drink, when there was a faint knock on my door. I opened it to our physical education teacher, and he handed me a letter and left. The letter contained information about a sexual education seminar after Sunday dinner for students between 14 and 16.

The weekend went slow. Lucy and I hung out, did some homework, wrote Dad a letter, rode our bikes around the streets, had fish 'n' chips, and played a few games of pinnies and a new arcade game called *Galaga*. In the meantime, I constantly wondered if I made the cut. Everyone ignored me at Sunday dinner when it was time for the seminar. The gang headed towards the hall together. Lucy and I walked in and were separated into groups. There must have been over a 100 of us in the hall.

There was a big screen, while the effervescent BJ and Principal Jones stood at the front, and the one I didn't like, Brother Emmanuel, watched on from the back, until footsteps could be heard, entering, echoing as they moved silently across the creaky boards. Without expression, he moved quietly towards the front, then stood before them.

'Today we are all gathered here to discuss and explain sex education.' BJ continued to speak while Brother Emmanuel handed out pamphlets and told us to watch the screen as this documentary-style film began.

I couldn't believe what I saw in the booklet: a man's penis and a woman's vagina. While I looked up the topic, the word 'masturbation' was echoing through the room, followed by the discussion of how babies were created. This all took my breath away, leaving me feeling a tad uncomfortable. Melissa peered at me with her usual smug smile, then began provocatively licking and sucking away on Chubba Chub lollypop; that shocked me a bit.

It dawned upon me how and why what was happening to me when I saw women I liked. BJ grabbed the microphone, addressing us.

'Okay, boys and girls. Today's sex education lesson is about teaching and learning about a broad variety of high-quality topics related to sex and sexuality. We will explore values and beliefs about those topics and skills that are required to navigate relationships while managing and understanding one's own sexual health.'

Murmurs and giggles stretched out through the room, fascinated by BJ, who was hushing everyone to be quiet. He began to address the students.

'Rights, respect, and responsibility,' he said, looking more serious than ever before. Reading from the screen above, he continued, 'Rights: Youth have the right to honest sexual health information; confidential, consensual sexual health services; and equitable opportunities to reach their full potential. Respect: Youth deserve respect. Valuing young people means authentically involving them in the design, implementation, and evaluation of programs and policies that affect their health and well-being. Responsibility: Society has the responsibility to provide young people with all of the tools they need to safeguard their sexual health, and young people have the responsibility to protect themselves.'

You could hear a pin drop, all eyes and ears on BJ. He captivated everyone and continued speaking, while on the screens photos and images appeared of a woman having a baby. There were also photos portraying sexually transmitted diseases, STDs. Photos of a man and woman engaging in sexual intercourse followed.

'Whoaaa, holy shit,' I spoke out loud.

I looked around to spot Melissa again, sitting with Tommy giggling together. Consumed by jealously, my focus went to finding my sister. I spotted her down by the front near Brother Emmanuel with other year-9 students.

'Now, health research shows us that comprehensive sex education provides young people with the essential information and skills they need to reduce their risk for unwanted pregnancy and STDs, including HIV.

'It can also help young people navigate puberty, understand the difference between healthy and unhealthy relationships, assisting to develop a healthy body image, promoting good communication and navigating the health care system. Quality sexuality education goes beyond the prevention of unwanted pregnancy and diseases to something much loftier, providing a life-long foundation for sexual health. Sexuality education can help shift a culture of fear, shame, and denial and in its stead begin to create one in which sexuality is accepted as a normal, natural, healthy part of being alive, of being a human; one in which young people are valued and celebrated for who they are, no matter their sexual orientation or gender identity or expression; and one in which sexual development is recognized as an important aspect of childhood and adolescence, and education about sexuality is valued over the promotion of ignorance.'

After about 30 minutes, the seminar ended with a few questions and answers. Walking out, I caught Melissa glancing at me. She quickly turned away and gave me no indication if I had made the audition.

I waited for Lucy. She asked how the audition went and if we had heard from Dad. We quickly caught up before Brother Emmanuel walked over, asking us to leave.

Later that night, I was anxious to know if I was in the band! I thought about Melissa all day and night. Learning something new at the seminar, I experimented with self-gratification. Turning the lights out, I cautiously placed my hands down my pants and began to touch myself, thinking of her. After a few minutes of pure pleasure and excitement of this new joy, the feeling was like a volcano about to explode out of my brains and my penis but felt amazing. I couldn't and didn't want to stop. It felt so wrong, but then again, it felt so good, until suddenly and surprisingly, a liquid spurted out of my penis. I gasped for air, astonished.

Delighted and content with myself, I was a man now. I was tickled pink. Melissa was on top of my list; I just had to convince her to see the light that I was a better guy than Tommy. Happily cleaning myself up, smiling like a Cheshire cat, and gathering my thoughts, I heard a noise like a twig break outside my window. I froze for a split second, my ears pricking up like a meerkat's.

Pulling the blinds across, I looked out to see a shadow disappear in the distance behind the trees into the darkness. A dog rustled around and looked for food as usual, peeing on a tree. Was it just the dog or somebody looking at me through my window? I become frightened and embarrassed, wondering who or what was out there, and more importantly, was this person looking and watching me, or was it just the dog wandering around?

Meanwhile, a young, inquisitive Lucy, climbed through The Creep's dorm window, snooping around and opening the wardrobe. She found a box. She quickly opened it to find some *Playball* and *Penthouse* magazines, random candles, ropes, and a Zippo lighter. Lucy flicked through casually while checking out the centerfold.

'Mmm, Miss April,' she says.

Suddenly, her ears pricked up to the sound of voices and keys rattling at the door. She returned the magazines, pocketed the silver Zippo lighter, closed the wardrobe, then climbed out the window just in the nick of time before The Creep walked in with a young boy following, his head down. Lucy spied on the man and witnessed what intrigued and excited her, also experiencing an immense feeling of hatred towards the man. They didn't explain this in the sex education seminar they had.

The next day, after a restless sleep of fidgeting, tossing, and turning in bed, I was determined to know if I had been chosen for the band. Music lessons were my second lesson for the day. I made my mind up to approach them. Meeting up with Lucy, she told me that I was in the band. She overheard Gaz and Dazza talking about it last night after the seminar. It was the best news ever. Still wanting confirmation, I wanted to hear straight from the horse's mouth.

I grabbed my vegemite on toast and walk towards a seat, with my sister looking around for the gang. They usually hung out together. Typically, there were about 200 plus kids in the cafeteria at any one time, but I couldn't see them. The chef was glaring at me while I was walking through the crowd, still not happy with me and the food fight I'd been blamed for.

Advanced English class quickly passed. Thank God, Mrs. Reeves kept busting my balls, giving me bad grades for short stories I had been writing, and failed my 500-word short story I had to write. Apparently, life on Mars isn't that cool in this school. I spent hours on that story and was not happy with her. For whatever reason, she had it in for me, and I didn't like her.

Racing to the music lessons, I observed everyone all together as I was walking into the room. Slowing down trying to act all cool calm and collected. They spotted me, darting into the room and taking their seats as if they owned the joint. More theory for the day and we had to play notes on a xylophone; this was killing me, so I asked Melissa if she had any news for me. She ignored me and went back to playing her chimes.

Looking around, I tried to get a signal or a sign from one of them. As the class finished, Melissa strutted up to me and said with authority, 'Practice is every Tuesday, Thursday, and Friday after school. If you miss one, you're out of the band.'

I was so ecstatic and overjoyed that I hugged her and gave her a big kiss on the cheek.

'Hey, settle down.' She pushed me away while the other guys looked on and gave me the nod of approval, except for Tommy, still unsure and furious.

'Melissa, get over here,' he said.

She flicked her hair back and headed back towards Tommy on his command.

Later, I found out Tommy was the hung vote who didn't want me in. Not caring anymore, I was in the band and closer to Melissa, if Tommy liked it or not. I had a feeling they were boyfriend and girlfriend. Still a little bit skeptical, I wanted to find out and clarify myself.

I was fired up. The first practice was more of a meeting and introduction of songs to learn and play. Becoming enthusiastic and mentioning the songs I knew; I explained my original songs and was eager to share with them. We all slowly placed our gear and positioned ourselves. Leigh had the upper hand arranging the amps, setting up microphones, fender guitar amps, and scattered leads around me, which had never happened before.

We set sail with a lengthy sound check, which also was a first for me. Twenty minutes or so passed, and I was ready and eager to explode. All the guys were taking time to set up and tuning one last time.

'Give us an E,' was the cry from Tommy, then the sounds or guitar strings, keys, and drums slowly filled the room with a thumping sound.

'Okay…one, two, three, four,' Tommy said.

I had no idea what we were about to play.

I followed, swiftly focusing on the chords and which notes to play.

'Twelve bar blues, guys, to warm up,' Tommy said.

'Love the blues,' I said to the members.

It was on: guitar riffs, heavy bass lines, hard smashing drums. Gazza reminded me of Animal from the Muppets. Tommy began his killer lead breaks and general jamming. I pulled out my harmonica and rattled off the most massive howling noise and bending notes, blending in with this raw sound while Leigh was mixing it up super well.

The jam went on for what felt like eight minutes or so when we wound it down. We all stopped, listened, and looked around at each other.

'That was awesome!' Tommy yelled, looking over toward his brother Leigh behind the desk.

I had a huge sigh of relief with a broad smile, trying to sus them both out.

"Rock 'n' Roll" by Led Zeppelin,' he said.

The sound of the wild guitar intro took off, followed by heavy drums alongside with ravaging bass. We were off again.

This was the beginning of the best moment of my life at the time. What would follow and what would happen next was beyond all our starry-eyed, ambitious, wannabe rock stars' wildest dreams.

We finally packed up. The guys all met, chatting in a group and then came to an agreement that I was officially a member of their band, and they told me to go back to their room for celebrations and a band meeting. Tommy and Melissa walked off, arm in arm, giggling and kissing and embracing each other.

I'd been waiting for this moment all my life. Collecting my gear and walking back to my room, I was chuffed and possessed a sense of pride about myself, thinking how my father and mother would feel right now. The sinking feeling that Melissa and Tommy were together was gut-wrenching, leaving me bat-crazy jealous, still trying my hardest to impress her.

Transfixed, I was watching Kids in the Kitchen perform their single, 'Change in Mood', live on *Countdown* when suddenly Lucy came charging in.

'Well?' A pause. 'What happened? Are you in the fucking band or what?' she squealed, jumping up and down with excitement.

'You bet your dog on it I am!' I embraced her, and we jumped around in circles, cheering and laughing.

Lucy nestled and nuzzled up next to me. We settled down, sitting on the end of the bed, she was sucking intently on a Red Skin lolly, checking out her new Zippo lighter.

'Where did you get that, Lucy?' I checked the bright flame come and go.

'I found it outside. You want it, Archie?'

'Sure, it's cool.' I flicked the Zippo lighter, intrigued 'This is it, Luc. This is all I ever have wanted to do.'

She took a big, deep breath. 'This is destiny. I can see the stars in your eyes, Archie.' She gave me cheeky nudge, making me fall of the end of the bed.

'Bloody hell, Lucy!' I popped back up, beaming.

She turned up the TV and looked at me with a huge cheeky grin as a *Countdown* promo clip was on.

'You're my hero bro, that'll be you one someday, Arch, playing live on *Countdown*. Dad will be so happy. You are born to play in a band and perform live on stage.'

A few minutes went by while flicking through some poems and songs that we had written until I remembered I had to go. I had written a few poems about Melissa, maybe even a love letter or two. I found it easier to write my feelings and how I felt, rather than saying them, keeping my raw emotions inside. Sadly, sometimes I held emotions in, especially anger that became toxically volcanic, erupting unexpectedly out of control at any given moment.

'I gotta fly, Luc. We're having a band meeting and celebrating, they reckon...'

'Ah, cool. Can I come?' she requested.

'I don't think so, sis. It's a band meeting, and I'm just keen to see how this goes, eh?'

I could see the let-down in her face and hear it in her tone of her voice.

'Oh, yeah, yeah, okay, no worries. Okay, well, you better not be late for your first meeting in that case.' She smiled, giving me another hug and kiss on the cheek. 'I'm so proud of you, bro. When are you going to tell the old man?'

'Tomorrow, sis. I'll buzz him tomorrow. See ya! I better go.'

We walked out of the room.

'Good luck,' she said.

We went our separate ways. I noticed her heading towards Brother Emmanuel's dorm. Chammy the dog was hanging around, sniffing for food as usual, cocking his leg on the small bush nearby.

I stopped to watch her knock on the door. He held out his hand, looking around. Lucy was compelled to follow the man inside his room, Chammy in tow, his tail wagging side to side happily. As he closed the door, he looked outside again. I didn't think much of it at the time. I didn't like that guy. We all adored the cute puppy always wanting to play and cuddle him. I ended up asking Lucy about her visits with Brother Emmanuel. She told me he was help-ing her with some English lessons. He did teach English as well, but I witnessed over time she did have many lessons with him.

Initiation

Arriving at Gazza and Dazza's room, I knocked on the door. Melissa opened the door. Her Joan Jett black hair was flawless and smelt amazing, like apple or musk; I couldn't put my finger on it.

'Quick, quick, get in,' she said, eyeing me up and down. Her cheeky smile made me weak at the knees.

Ushered in, I smelled smoke in the back room.

'This way.' She gently pushed the small of my back.

Entering the smoke-hazed room, *Countdown* was on the tele, turned down. On the walls were posters of Bruce Lee, Led Zeppelin, Rolling Stones, Holden Monaro, and Elle Macpherson from *Sports Illustrated* in a bikini. I instantly gravitated to the last one.

A roar came from the guys sitting there sharing a smoke and knocking back some drinks. An empty packet of Samboy salt and vinegar chips ruffled on the floor next to scrunched-up empty packet of Winnie Blue ciggies, and few boys played a game of cards.

'Ace high, twenty-one!' Daz yelled with glee, throwing the cards down and sweeping a handful of coins scattered on the table, looking extremely happy with himself, ripping open a Polly waffle, which was gone in three bites.

'You're kidding me,' his brother said, surprising himself, flicking a ciggie into his mouth and lighting it up.

The sweet song, 'Ballroom Blitz', blasted on the record player, filling the room with a festive ambience.

'Cheers, Archie, come on in. Have some of this,' Leigh requested, dancing away to the song, passing me a can of beer.

'It's okay, guys. I don't smoke or drink. Makes me a bit ill,' I explained.

The guys busted out in laughter.

'Fuck off, mate! This is part of your initiation. To become a fully-fledged member, bro,' Daz said. As he stood up from his card game, he knocked over some coins and laughed at himself. He passed me the smoke rolled up in a small cigarette and stuffed his face with more potato chips, spitting half of them out in mid-laughter. Specks of chips splattered on my face.

Wiping his disgusting mess off me, I addressed the group that I didn't smoke ciggies and shrugged. I noticed the guys had money on the table, cards, and dice.

'Well, that's okay, mate, because this isn't ciggies,' Daz said.

They continued to laugh.

Giving into the peer pressure, I accepted a puff of the smoke, which was some marijuana mixed with a little cigarette. Taking a drag or two, I inhaled and instantly coughed, losing my breath, gagging.

'Here you go, mate. Have a drink of this,' Gaz said, handing me a bottle.

I wasn't sure what it was. It had a big skull. I found out it was bourbon. I spurted a bit of it out.

'What the hell?!' I said, trying to get my breath again, wiping the spillage from my mouth. It took me a few minutes to get myself together. 'When we starting the meeting?'

'This is the meeting, cowboy,' Tommy said as he passed another smoke to me and gingerly handed me a beer. His shoulder still had not fully recovered from the gunfire that shattered his scapula bone.

'A toast to Arhcie,' Gaz said, clinking his beer bottle at mine. A freshly squeezed zit still had some puss seeping from it, which made me squeamish. He took a swig, then unleashed an unholy belch directly in my face that nearly made me puke.

'Oh, boy, that's gross,' I whispered to myself.

Going along and having a few more puffs and skulling the beer on their instructions, I followed with a colossal belch to the cry and joy from the others. Not long after this, the room began moving. I looked at a card on the table. On the cover was a picture of a small dog. I was fascinated by this picture, when suddenly,

Tommy rushed up behind me, barking like a dog. He scared the hell out of me!

'Holy smoke, Tommy!' I yelled, nearly crapping myself.

He laughed uncontrollably, followed by the others. I joined in the hysterical laughter for a minute or two. I had no sense of time.

'Wow,' I said in disbelief. 'What in the hell is going on?' I reached for the packet of plain potato chips.

'Cowboy's got the munchies. Let's get pizza,' Daz said to the chorus of agreement from the gang.

A scene of uncontrollable laughter, jokes, beers, singing, eating, and dancing to the record collection and more smokes continued for the next few hours. Melissa and Tommy had left together after making out on the couch for over an hour. Leigh was passed out on the couch. Gazza and Daz were transfixed on their card game.

'What are you playing?' I asked curiously.

'Blackjack,' they chimed in sync. They were wearing matching turquoise floral paisley short-sleeved tight shirts, deliberately showing of their bulging biceps. Bizarre.

'Twins, eh?' I mumbled to myself. 'What's blackjack?'

'I'm gonna make him an offer he can't refuse,' Gaz said, giggling as he quoted the Godfather. He attempted an Italian mafia god voice, placing his hands under his mouth whilst speaking, taking another drag of his ciggie, blowing four perfect smoke rings.

They both filled me in on the rules. The aim was to beat the banker and get twenty-one or ace high with a picture card or ten called blackjack. Joining in for a few hands, about an hour passed. The odds were stacked up against me. Getting to know the twins a little better was worthwhile losing my dough. I decided it was best to go back to my dorm.

A little while later, I lay in my room. With no warning, it started spinning. My head was twirling and twisting, like a cyclone had appeared out of nowhere. Feeling ill, unable to lie down anymore, I raced to the bathroom and became violently ill. This continued until I had nothing left in the tank and was left dry-retching. The smell was disgusting. I had never felt this dreadful in all my life.

One lesson I thought I would have learnt from my mistake. It was the start of a journey riddled with recklessness, booze, drugs, sex, crime, but best of all, rock 'n' roll and good times.

Performance

The morning chimes of the bells echoing through the campus woke me up. I turned the

TV onto the news with Prime Minister Bob Hawke telling everyone: 'If your boss sacks you today, you're a bum.' He then laughed out loud. We had just won some yacht race called the America's Cup one year ago to the day, the sports reporter was talking about it, and how the Aussies beat the Americans was all the rage. I became a little captivated while they showed off the keel, with a guy called Alan Bond behind this unique keel. I remember it had been on all over the news last year.

It was a proud time to be an Aussie in the mid-'80s. They even changed our national anthem from 'God Save the Queen' to 'Advance Australia Fair' in 1984. I thought 'Waltzing Matilda' would have been a good one. Dad used to play that sometimes at gigs.

In VFL, South Melbourne ventured up to Sydney, soon to become the Sydney Swans with this eccentric high-flying blond full-forward wearing tight shorts, Warwick Capper. In the schoolyard or at footy practice, we would try and take a specki and yell out 'Capper!'

Switching the tele off, I flicked on the radio. Bananarama's 'I'm Your Venus' was on. I ad-libbed, singing, 'I'm your penis.' Over time, the gang and I had pretty well become friends.

We would go to the park ride on the BMX track and get our skateboards. We all played football, cricket, or some form of sport. Tommy was one of the best footy players in our school, a natural all-rounder sportsman. We used to have 100-metre races. I only beat him once out of five times, but the music was our all-time passion and the favourite thing that we all had in common.

Our relationship was like chalk and cheese; opposites attract. He liked Collingwood. I liked North Melbourne. He played ruck changing in the backline; I played rover and in the forward line. He played electric guitar. I played acoustic. He liked vanilla; I liked chocolate. One thing was clear what we had in common was we both liked Melissa.

Tommy and Leigh's parents were real estate agents, working six days a week, based in Essendon. They decided it was best for them to go to the school rather than public school. Mel's parents separated. Her mother placed her in the school. Her dad had a criminal record and was facing some time in prison for assault. Gaz and Daz's parents lived out in Ballarat working in the gold mine fourteen days on and seven days off.

We did some petty crime: break-and-enters into nearby shops and houses, stealing whatever we could get our hands on. Who says 'crime doesn't pay?' My biggest score was $480 cash in a house three blocks away. We had a massive party that night. In shops, we took simple items, like bags of chips, chocolate bars, and lollies. That's how it started, anyway.

One top money spinner was to steal books and sell them to second-hand bookstores. Another was to collect cans and empty bottles, taking them to the recycle depot nearby. We would find a way to make ends meet and have enough money for fish 'n' chips, video, plus pinball games. Lucy would write poetry, draw pictures of angels and sketches, while somehow my sister always had access to money. Buying clothes, shoes, makeup, and whatever she wanted made me curious. Her demeanour was changing daily.

Lucy came up with some crazy business ideas. One was like Maxwell Smart's shoe phone; she wanted a phone where you could go anywhere with it. We all told her she was crazy, but she said we were all stupid and genuinely believed it was a great idea. Secretly, I thought it was a good idea as well.

It was time to get ready for practice yet again. We rehearsed day after day, getting ourselves prepared for the Battle of the Bands comp. We had to submit two recordings, and if we were successful at winning first place, we would be invited to play at the local youth festival with some of Australia's finest bands, and rumours were that INXS were headlining this year.

Our music and attitude now seemed to gel and fit into place. If we weren't at school, which was between 9 a.m. to 4 p.m., or not in detention, it was music lessons 24/7. We met in the music room after school to practise and kept on jamming until we felt tired and or had enough of each other.

By now, the bond was planted like the Garden of Eden. Even when tempted and watered, everybody seemed to mould and knew precisely when one's time was to shine then contribute. We created some form of a musical masterpiece we were all pleased and happy with the result, as Leigh had mastered our sound and had some excellent recordings. Don't get me wrong; we all had our own specific personalities and voiced strong opinions.

I had an inkling Tommy was still unsure about me and was always keen on Melissa. I was not too fond of the way he talked to her, sometimes yelling at her, demanding she do this or that. I wished she were with me and not him.

'I know we're ready; our tracks are solid as,' Gaz said.

'I'm not sure, bro. I mean, we have a few covers and a couple of originals down.' His brother responded.

'We can tighten up and collaborate the verses and especially the chorus. If this is going to be one of the first tracks we ever record or perform, I don't know about you, man, but I prefer we nail it, then add all the bullshit behind it.'

'Let's write it, then build it. We have all the resources here,' Daz said.

We had practised and jammed until we all felt tired and sick of each other, arguing, bickering, all very restless, all very hungry. We packed up for the night. Daz invited me back for a feed that I reluctantly agreed to.

'Meet you there, okay?' I said, absolutely starving. It could be chicken lungs for all I cared.

I went back to Daz's dorm. He was cooking away, trying to copy and read carefully out of a cooking book. In the background on the record player was some classic howling blues.

'Who's this, Daz?' I asked, walking towards the vinyl.

'Sonny Terry and Brownie McGee, mate,' he said.

'Oh, cool,' I said, fascinated with the old timer's music and checking out the cover. 'What you cooking, mate?' I ask sniffing, while thinking when the next rehearsal was.

'Relax, Max,' he said, swiftly manoeuvring through his kitchen area, imitating the Swedish chef from the Muppets. He diced and tossed ingredients while headfirst in his cookbook, moving from the bench top to his round saucepan.

'What the heck are you doing, man?' I asked, witnessing noodles, a variety of vegetables, and meat flying and spinning through the air back into the saucepan, smoke filling the air.

'This is our dinner, mate. Singapore noodle,' he explained, modestly flipping and stirring constantly. He kept looking at me with a quirky smirk, thinking he was cooking something special. It smelt great, though.

'What? You're sending all the wrong signals, man. Mixed messages,' I said.

He just smiled.

'We been offered by Brother John to perform three songs at an interim lunch for the senior grades' family function.'

Instantly, our fixed eyes, wide open with surprise. Fear, admiration, bewilderment, horror, and curiosity loomed.

'Bull dust.' I gulped, pondering the thought of my father being here and reflecting on my mother's tragedy. I was feeling mystified and blank.

'Well,' Daz asked, 'what the fuck you reckon?' He served up my noodles, spilling them all over the bowl and table.

'When?' I asked.

'Two weeks, next Friday,' he replied.

'Do the other guys know?' I asked.

'Not yet. I only found out on the way here. BJ pulled me up quickly. He heard us jamming and just came out with it. I had to tell someone, man. I was busting at the seams. I wanted to eat quickly, then announce it to the others. So, eat up and let's break the news.'

Once we were all together for the first rehearsal for our first live performance, the tone and mood had slipped from upbeat energy to a light, loose, comfortable indoor synergy to an erratic and slippery, elusive motion that could not sliver into a regular rhythm or tune.

A whole lot of noise and not much music was the outcome.

'Wait up, wait up.' Lucy seemed forthcoming, walking between the band's space, waving her hands and intervening.

'I have heard you guys play this lick and rhythm before; it's a twelve-bar blues riff. Why not add your own unique polished manner upon it? So, in 20 years' time people will still be playing it, and you'll get paid royalties every time it's aired on the radio, TV, wherever.

'Instead of bands playing Beatles or Rolling Stones covers, they'll cover ours. You have to think like that. Otherwise, you'll be nothing, just another garage band doing the same old pub gigs, and I'm not wasting my time for anything.' She went on a bit as an uneasy rest hovered, filling the room.

I could feel the tension.

'What the hell is she going on about, covering our songs?' Melissa asked.

'Hear me out. You do this, then we submit for the Battle of the Bands.'

'There is no "we" Lucy,' Melissa said.

We all stopped and looked around the room at each other, wondering, *What the hell?*

'Let me manage you guys,' Lucy stated. 'You can count on me. I can push and pull you, even get you gigs as well. I've met some people.'

'I don't think you know what you're talking about,' Tommy dismissed her.

'I'm not sure, Lucy. We will have a think and have a band meeting, okay?' Melissa said, followed a chorus of agreement. She looked at me.

I couldn't resist and had to stick up for my sister. 'We will need a manager if we want to make it big. INXS and the other bands have a manager. She does make a lot of sense. We are doing what everyone else is doing, and we need to be a bit different from the rest and stand out.'

'Yes.' Lucy was getting more excited and dramatic now. 'More significant harmonies, bigger sound, even add some electronica in there. I hear rap is in at the moment.'

'Screw rap! Dazza yelled.

'Yeah, well, do you like the Sex Pistols?' Lucy cut in.

'Yeah,' we all agreed.

'Well, the manager of them released that song "Three Buffalo Girls", and it's rap. They feature break dancers, and it's just made top five in the USA.'

That's when the lightbulb moment struck us. None of us wanted Lucy representing us, not even me, but she just made so much sense. For her being a 15-year-old, she was more business-minded than any of us.

'We'll think about it,' Tommy agreed. 'Now, can you leave us be for now, so we can rehearse, Lucy?'

I nodded and gestured towards the door to my sister.

'Justice will be done,' she said on her way out, giving us the peace sign, then flipped it around quickly to me.

Lucy could feel her shady plans derailing, leading her down a dark path filled with uncertainty and anxiety.

Freshly inspired hours went by, playing, writing, swapping licks, leads, and heading towards our first performance. We had to perform three songs as the finale of the luncheon. It was time, and we hadn't even a name for the band.

There was no turning back now, the moment of truth.

'Bugger this,' Leigh said, setting up the leads.

Leigh's sound check went well, but it was to an empty auditorium. Now that same auditorium was bursting with students. The vice principal was on stage; my heart raced like a V8, my throat collapsed, and my nerves nearly made me faint. We were introduced as The High School Band. We looked at each other and made our moves to our instruments. Initially, there was silence in the room. There must have been 300 people sitting down, just looking at us. Barely able to breathe, I felt comfortable and a sense of belonging on stage, until my knees buckled. I heard a massive roar of the count.

'One...two...three!' Gazza called out, his sticks smashing together.

The bass fired up, drums kicked in; I closed my eyes and played some chords until we were all in time and tune.

Taking an almighty deep breath, I began to sing the song I wrote called 'Carefully Sold', bringing in the verses, then the chorus, 'Trusting our Bridge'. By then, it all fell into place, and we all rocked as hard as we could to finish the song. The last chord was strummed, a group of notes combined according to some system, then gently faded out to a peaceful end. I was on such a high, filled with adrenalin.

'We are the band!' I yelled and was receipted to applause, cheers, and whistles from the audience.

The 300-plus crowd of students were all screaming, yelling for more, while I did notice the brothers, some parents and the principal glare or frown. We must have committed a mortal sin, but

I had no idea what blasphemy I had just spoken sacrilegiously about God or other sacred things.

On the other hand, a distinctive feeling of elation came across me. I pulled out my harmonica from my back pocket and began to huff and puff like a werewolf, ripping out 'The Train'. The sound of drums followed, along with bass, keys, and Tommy's wickedly fantastic guitar solo on his pride-and-joy 1972 Fender Stratocaster, or the 'Srat' as Tommy called it. It was arguably the most iconic and most copied guitar design of all time, scorching through his lovely 1963 VOX AC30 vintage fender amp, featuring new griller cloth and tolex, vintage silver VOX speakers.

We were now all officially loose and at ease and introduced our version of twelve-bar blues. We had some lyrics we had experimented with and didn't want the song to end. We didn't want that moment to end at all. We wrapped it up playing the classic Rolling Stones song, 'Sympathy for the Devil', that we had rehearsed time and time again. It went for over ten minutes. Again, I was ripping out my harp, blasting and bending notes. Tommy bended strings, tearing out wicked lead breaks. The whole auditorium sang as well; the crowd interaction was unreal.

'Pleased to meet you. Hope you guess my name.'

'Whoo, whoo, whoo, whoo!' They all joined in as part of the song. The sound was excellent.

Looking over towards Leigh, I gave him a huge smile. He returned with a thumbs-up, poking his head up behind the desk and greeted me with a warm, distinctive smile.

The vice principal was winding us up, as thanks to us, the lunch hour had already been overly extended. We walked off the stage, heads held high, high-fiving each other; the room was electric.

The vice principal came back on the stage, thanked us, 'The Band,' then ordered everyone to get back to class, as we had held everyone up. So, that was it. The first thing we all agreed on was how awesome that was, then secondly, we had to come up with a name for the band.

We had to pack up as quickly as we could to get back to class. When entering the room, my English teacher welcomed me back as 'the rock star.'

'I wonder if he'll be late for any other gigs,' she stated, smiling.

The class began to laugh at me. I made my way to my chair, sinking and suffering in my silence. Bit too close to the bone. I just entertained the other students, teachers, and families, and for the first time ever, I expressed myself naturally, especially my music. Being ridiculed, becoming fully aware of showing my music to express myself and giving up my soul was like giving up a limb or a piece of the human body. It was true. I just sold my soul for rock 'n' roll.

Wondering to myself and taking a deep breath, I angrily stood up.

'What I have achieved with the group of people and band I'm in, your negativity or words will not arouse any effect or evoke any specific functional emotion within me at all.'

'Archie, sit down,' Mrs. Reeves snapped.

'I have extreme patience and tolerance, and I'm more than 100% confident that what the school witnessed today, you will see again, and we will raise more awareness.' Turning back to the teacher, I stared her straight in the eyes, just like she asked me to and said, 'And with no disrespect, we will earn more money from our songs than you, or this school will make in a lifetime.'

The class sniggered, talking amongst themselves.

Some cheered and some yelled abuse. 'Loser!' 'You're a dick-head, cowboy!' 'Wanker!'

Dodging some crunched-up paper, I headed straight to the guy who threw it at me. The teacher intervened, demanding I sit down.

'Silence, sit down now!' the teacher ordered. 'In fact, Archie, you have a lot to say, so it's your time to read.'

I was so pissed off as I turned back to my desk. The girl in front of me was smiling. I noticed her before. She was cute as she lifted her eyebrows and looked at me, waiting.

Managing a huge sigh, I opened the book to continue reading, my heart racing again. Muttering and mumbling, I was nervous, mispronouncing words, not even able to finish sentences. This was humiliating. I wanted to march out of the room. Guess we can call that one even between the teacher and me.

I wanted to know this girl. I'd seen her around with her girl-friends, and they were all pretty cute, giving me looks and smiles that have nearly knock be down before. In a blink of an eye, one of the students had thrown a pencil case into the fan. Feeling the breeze from the fan, the thunderous whizzing sound passed my ear. I ducked for cover, and the blade came flying out and whacked her fair square on the head, knocking her unconscious.

The classroom erupted, trying to identify the culprit. The siren went. Everyone scampered to race out of the room, except a couple of her friends and myself, making sure she was all right. Blood seeped from her right eyebrow. She was clearly not okay. The medics came in while quickly ushering the rest of us out of the room. Shell-shocked was one way to describe what just happened.

I looked up towards the teacher.

'You're going to detention, Archie.'

'But—'

'But nothing,' she cut in, pointing to the door. 'Now.'

The Creep

More than ever, time had flown very quickly. Studying was harder. Jamming kind of took a back step for a bit. My grades were poor, and I had plenty of struggles.

Lucy was having a variety of issues of her own, turning into a young teenage woman. One specific day, she noticed her first period while in the shower. Panicking, she thought she was dying, running around the campus, half-naked in a towel, screaming, 'I'm dying, I'm dying!' until a nun attended to her, calming her down and explaining her situation. The nun took her away into medical.

I heard about the unconventional behaviour and went to visit her. 'Lucy?' I knocked on the door. 'Are you okay?'

'Yeah, I'm fine, just leave me alone.'

'Don't be so hard on yourself, sis.'

'Leave me alone, for God's sake, Archie,' she said. She fell quiet as the nuns helped her.

'God works in mysterious ways, Lucy,' the nun consoled her while four other very dignified sisters looked on, taking solemn vows, praying, and holding onto their rosaries. 'A child needs their mother,' the nun said. 'We will pray the joyful mysteries now.'

They gathered around a painting of Mother Teresa of Calcutta situated in the middle of the wall.

'You're turning into a young woman, Lucy. Your mother will be so happy for you.' The nun caressed the frightened young girl's soft, cold, trembling hands. 'It's okay to have some secrets, Lucy; we all have them.'

The other sisters agreed.

'Yes, yes, we all have them,' one repeated while she continued to hold her rosary, praying.

'We can hide them in passageways,' another said. 'You will be fine, Lucy. No seclusion room for you today.'

I stood in silence and watched this moving scene unfold.

Lucy was forthcoming and becoming a spoiled little bitch, in and out of trouble, becoming so rebellious it was doing my head in. But she was my sister, and I loved her regardless. We found out someone was writing graffiti on the school walls and surrounding areas that she was a slut, mole, bitch, and all sorts of degrading comments and diagrams. She was distraught and angry by the derogatory comments made about her, which was a psychological burden, including random small outbursts of anger. She was getting in more trouble and having some fights with boy and girl students. She often hung out with the older students, instead of kids her own year.

Trying her best at school, she was always on edge. Lucy seemed to be desperately trying to rid herself of her emotional wounds, frightened they would remain, scarring her for the rest of her life. I decided it was best to leave her alone.

Incidents like this one put her right back in the shit. She had regular counselling, one day a week, for four weeks with a clinical social worker. My sister had become very anxious, dark like poison ivy, defenseless, and open for attack. She blamed me for the position she was in and the lack of limitation and joy. She would tell me that she felt insecure, in need of protection, and had no support here.

Not long ago, she was sent to medical for slicing her wrists with a small shaver's blade; later that same day, she was seen on top of the cafeteria roof just standing there, motionless, until one of the sisters climbed up and talked her down.

Dad's visits and letters were becoming less often now for whatever reason. It broke my heart to see my sister like this.

Witnessing Mother's death sent her into a state of sudden and intense overpowering emotion that had taken its toll on her. It was hard for to seek fulfillment, while I had found it easy. Her mind was sometimes ecstatic, then suddenly become erratic. Like a flick of a switch, she snapped.

The math's teacher sent her to Vice Principle Dixon for writing on her desk 'By the powers of evil, I have smelt the breath of Satan and heard the demons' voices - cold, scratchy, dead voices carrying messages of hatred through my mind. Jesus is more interested in power than in saving souls.'

It was seriously something straight out of the movie, *The Exorcist*.

In the library, I had come across an article in a London paper that read:

'In churches and parochial schools alike, the subject of Hell is avoided, as one Midwestern priest put it, in order not to put people on a guilt trip. The idea of sin is likewise avoided, in order not to do irreparable damage to what has been taught for the past fifteen years.

'When the rebellion of the possessed person does lead to exorcism, the bitter struggle is brought out into the open,' he wrote. 'The Exorcist offers himself as a hostage.'

It kind of spooked me out about it. I wondered if Lucy was possessed; she certainly at times acted like it.

One day, I saw Lucy come out of the dorm of the one of the brothers, The Creep. He always went on about 'the seven deadly sins' and how the Catholic Church used the concept of the deadly sins to help people curb their temperament towards evil before dire repercussions and misdeeds could occur.

The leader-teachers primarily focused on pride, which is thought to be the sin that severs the soul from grace and the one that is representative of the very essence of all evil and greed. Both are inherently seen as sinful and as underlying all other sins to be prevented. The brother was preaching this to us often. I figured it would be an alright name for our band, 'Seven Deadly Sins' or the 'The Deadly Sins.'

He was a creepy, shady old man. Just the thought of going into his room made the hair on the back of my neck stand up. Lucy was looking deeply upset, often wiping tears from her face. The changes taking place in her were noticeable. After a long moment, on my tippy toes, I snuck into his dorm and found him with a student kneeling in front of him. I was greeted by Chammy barking at me. He was surprised when he turned his head to see me standing there in disbelief and demanded that I get out. I wanted to know what the kid was doing kneeling in front of him. He claimed that he was praying and making confessions of his sins, and if I didn't leave, he would tell the principal that Lucy was selling drugs to other students and that we would be kicked out of the school.

'What are you talking about, ya creep?' I asked, shaking my head in dismay.

'Ask your sister.' He gave me an evil, wry smile. 'I caught her selling cannabis to one of the students. Not to mention seeing her off campus after curfew. I am happy to inform the principal, and you will be both kicked out of school,' he threatened. 'Get out!' he screamed, pointing to the door.

I knew I didn't like this guy for a reason; he was a creepy old man, and even his long, lanky finger looked like a twig from an old tree.

'As a matter of fact, you can come to see me as well, Archie Saunders.' His voice sounded creepier than usual. An array of ropes around his bedside and candles glowing in the background caught my eye as I made my way out.

Frantically searching for my sister, I couldn't find her anywhere. Waiting in her room, I eventually drifted off to asleep. The lights switching on woke me up, startling me.

'Where the hell have you been?' I demanded.

She returned hours later, just after 3 a.m. 'At a friend's house.' Her voice was quivering.

'Where are you making all your money? Why are you wearing makeup? Where have you been, Lucy?'

She told me not to worry about her. She seemed agitated, coy, and not interested. I explained what happened at the brother's dorm. She denied everything.

She wanted to go to bed and asked me to leave. I was going to get to the bottom of whatever was going on.

'Stop busting my chops, Archie. It's none of your business.'

I grabbed her arm as she tried to walk away. 'What's happening, Lucy?'

'Fuck off!' she screamed, yanking her arm away. 'Leave me alone.'

'Tell me,' I demanded.

'Fuck you.'

'No, fuck you,' I bit back.

Head down and rubbing her hands over her face, she broke down. 'You weren't there, Archie!'

'Where?' I replied, puzzled.

'On Sally, the horse accident when Mum died. I saw it happen in front of me.'

'Ah, sis.' I placed my arm around her shoulder.

'I have nightmares nearly every night about it. I see Mum in the distance and run to her when there is no one there. I speak with her sometimes. Just leave me alone.'

Trying to console her, she shrugged me off and stormed out of her room, the door slam echoing throughout the campus. Sitting back on the bed, I wanted to cry and get the hell out of here. The painful memories flooded back. I missed Dad and my dog. I knelt and said a little prayer.

'Dear God, please look after Mum and give guidance to Lucy. Mum, if you're listening, I hadn't been with you long enough to know everything about you, but I had been with you enough to love and miss you dearly. Death doesn't change you because you're always going to be an angel in our lives. Dad, if you can hear me, you are my best friend, my hero, my rock. I miss you. Rusty, you are my best mate. I miss our cuddles, our playtime, and I just miss you with all my heart and more than anything in the world. Amen.'

The sound of ambulance sirens woke me up. I found it hard to get back to sleep. A shadow disappeared from my window. The sirens of an ambulance kept me awake. I rested my head and decided to look out the window towards the sky. I followed the sounds that were trying to escape my mind, chasing them along the way down the street... A shining light and a familiar sound out my bedroom window caught my attention. 'Chammy,' I said, peering through the window, noticing a comet or a shooting star. Nothing was there.

The Creep

Night Out

Lying in bed having cuddles with Chammy, the dog's white face was cluttered with dirt. I was watching the Cheech and Chong video, *Up in Smoke*, enjoying a packet of Chicken Chickadee's, washing it down with a can of TAB. The TV commercial worked, featuring Elle MacPherson. What a body! Then there was a vigorous banging on my door. The gang stormed in, jumped onto my bed, and scuffed my hair and head like jelly. In an obsession of frenzy, all the fellas jumped onto the bed, wildly humping my body and leg. Cham was barking at them, wagging his little fluffy tail. Leigh was dry-humping the dog, howling.

'That's gross!' I yelled with a mouthful of chips.

Poor little Cham leapt off the bed and legged it out of there, his tail between his legs.

Watching the video, all of us laughed and imitated Cheech and Chong from the car scene being pulled up by the cops, stupidly in sync together, giggling and humping, ferociously united. I cried out for help, followed by relentless laughter and retaliation.

'We killed it yesterday, Archie,' Gaz said, smelling of alcohol and dope. The gross yellow bottom tooth he had that stank like dog shit. His acne was getting worse. Freshly picked zits all over his chin and face were putrid.

'Get off,' I pleaded, holding off the smile until we all wrestled each other. We were celebrating our first live performance our specific way - our style. It was just after 9 p.m. on a crispy Friday night and a full moon.

'Come on, let's go,' Daz said. 'There is a blue light disco on tonight, so grab Luc. Let's sneak out of here and go to the bottlo', then the park.' He showed off a small bag of grass.

'You guys are Cheech and Chong,' I told them, grinning ear to ear. 'Let's leave my little sister out of this, though, yeah?'

'Ah, get stuffed.' Daz scoffed, searching for his Winnie Blues.

The gang argued whether to get her to join in the celebrations, discussing which bottlo' we should hit.

'Come off it, guys; she's only 15. Leave her be; she will be asleep anyway.'

I knew Daz liked her. I wanted her to be with us, to join in on the glory of enjoying the moment. However, I was thinking of Dad and how Mum would have felt.

'Forget it!' I yelled out to a chorus of boos and heckles. 'Stop picking on me, you guys. Let's go.'

We started shuffling the lads towards the door. We were on the prowl, walking on eggshells out of the campus to the Errol Street bottlo' before we were destined to cause chaos at the blue light disco. We had technique stealing from bottle shops. Tommy, the eldest, would buy a flagon of Moselle or a six-pack of beers, something cheap. Melissa would be by his side. The attendant would be focused on her. Meanwhile, Gaz and I would walk in, acknowledging the attendant, while Dazza would go in, unexpected. The twins would confuse and distract the attendant while I would grab one bottle of whatever was on offer. Never greedy, just one bottle at a time. We had to work each bottle shop differently and would wait a month or so before shopping at the same store. On tonight's menu was a small bottle of Milne's whiskey and Mezcal tequila.

We smoked up a bit, shared whiskey, and tequila washed it down with a cheap flagon of Moselle. It tasted disgusting.

'Ewww, there's a bloody worm in here,' Mel said after taking a hefty slug of tequila.

'I'll eat that,' Leigh jumped in.

'Gross.' She grimaced.

All of us sang, danced, sculled, yelled, screamed, and howled at the full moon shining down upon us.

'Watch this move.' Gaz wanted the spotlight. He attempted some form of break dance, then moonwalk, to a round of applause, followed by an attempt of a Tarzan beating his chest.

'Shut up, Gaz,' his brother told him.

'No, you shut up.'

'You shut up.'

'No, you shut up.'

They continued, laughing at one another, doing their best impersonation, imitating the Fonz from *Happy Days*.

'Ehhhh,' Gaz said, giving us all the both thumbs-up.

Daz slapped his brother on the back of his head, acting like the skipper from *Gilligan's Island*.

I started singing the theme song from *Gilligan's Island*, secretly trying to impress Melissa. They all joined in the chorus. Melissa reminded me a little of Marian. She was my favourite.

We were having a fat time. I hadn't had a good laugh in weeks, until Dazza, out of nowhere, grabbed a rock and threw it at the local fish 'n' chip shop window.

'Holy shit, bro,' Gaz said. 'What the hell? Let's go.'

A massive piercing, shattering sound echoed throughout the clear, chilly night. Alarms went off. We panicked, running through the park towards the road, stumbling and tripping over the curbs. Bouncing back up, I grazed my elbow, also taking some skin off my hands and knuckles. It stung like hell.

To make matters worse, as I was slowly getting up, Leigh ran past and pushed me back down into the asphalt, laughing along the way. Tommy jumped over me like a rolling, stoned Giselle. Suddenly, I was circled by the group, or more like a pack of wolves in this full moon, until the sirens and bright lights shone directly on me like a deer. I froze.

'Run!' Tommy yelled.

We bolted towards the bushes while two police cars drove up to the fish 'n' chip shop, investigating the window and mess we made. The police officers began to shine their lights all around the park and towards the bushes.

I was so scared that the combination of the whiskey, cheap wine, and grass made my head start to spin. I vomited into the bushes while Tommy burst into laughter, making the other guys start to giggle. They broke into hysterical laughter. Wiping vomit from my mouth and face, I was disgusted; however, I joined in laughing and giggling like a typical school kid, squinting in the dark, trying to hide from the cops, and smiling while wiping my face. It was horrible.

The guys were all rolling around the bushes, trying to hide and keep quiet. Tears poured out of our eyes until a bright light shone right on us.

'I've seen the light,' Gaz said.

We broke into hysterics again. To our despair, it was two officers shining the lights at us.

'Freeze!' What's going in there, guys? Come out with your hands up, slowly.'

Those words were the sternest I had ever heard. On all fours, crawling out of the bush, we gathered our composure. The others took off sprinting across the park with two police officers chasing them. I was not in a good place, and my head was spinning 100 miles an hour. My stomach was ill; the sky was spiraling out of control. I sweated more than ever before.

'Put your hands on your head,' one officer demanded.

'What's your name?' the officer asked me with the torch directly on my face while his other hand grasped his revolver.

Unable to speak, I felt sick.

His was a familiar face. He yelled out again.

I came to terms with the fact the others had run away, leaving me on my own.

He approached me with his hand armed on his gun holster. Throwing up all over the policeman, I buckled onto my hands and knees. The last thing I recalled was a big bang. Was I shot, or had I gone straight to Hell?

Waking up on a hard bench, my mouth was dry. A foul taste of stale alcohol and vomit lingered. Squinting through a bunch of brass in the dark, I wondered what happened last night. The last thing I remembered was howling at the moon.

A guy being dragged along by three policemen caught my eye. He was motionless, groaning. Having no clue what happened the night before, my body ached all over, especially my ribs. It felt like a couple had cracked; my head thumped. Hours slowly dragged on. I was fed some food, which was a highlight: cheese and old, stale crackers plus water.

An officer tapped on the bars with his baton, informing me that I had a visitor. Apprehensive and sore, a million thoughts and memories rattled through my brain. I had been locked up for over 24 hours.

The warden opened the cell, instructing me to put my hands between the bars.

Responding swiftly to his command, I was handcuffed for the first time I could remember.

'You have a visitor, pal,' he snarled, 'but believe me, you would be safer staying in here, I reckon.'

His snarl turned into a cynical smile as he forced me up along the hallway, pushing the steel baton in the small of my spine, whacking the back of my head for good measure. I was escorted to the window where Father waited. My hands went to my head. I felt so sick, confused and wanting to throw up again. His normally hazel eyes turned to a dark brown, glistening red and were bloodshot. I knew damn well he was furious.

'Hmmm, Archie.' He sighed, shaking his head. 'I'm not a happy man. I have no idea what I am doing here. I get a phone call at 11 p.m. last night, waking me up. They told me that you were drunk and disorderly, vomited on a police officer, and assaulted another, broke his nose, for crying out loud.

'I'm disappointed right now. I have driven all night. Your stupidity has cost me more than I can afford in bail. I was hoping, no, praying that sending you to the private Catholic school would give you the education that would benefit you for your future. Then, I hear about break-and-enters, theft, vandalism, drunkenness, and disorderliness, plus assault charges. Mate, you're only 16, for crying out loud. What were you thinking?'

No memory any of that happening, I thought in absolute disbelief.

'Your mother would be so upset if she were here.'

A mental image of a smashing window in the fish 'n' chips shop popped into my head. I loved that shop; it has the best fish 'n' chips. We hung out there playing video games and pinball every weekend. Part of my parole ended up having to do 20 hours of community work back at the fish 'n' chip shop on weekends.

Hanging my head in disgrace and shame, I began to tear up, then sobbed helplessly. Dad paid the bail. Without being aware of how much, I was barely able to walk and limped. My ribs and arms ached, and sore all over nursing a massive headache to boot. Released from the watch-house, I gingerly walked out of the station. A voice spoke in the background.

'You're a marked man now, cowboy.'

I felt like a dog with his tail between his legs. I took a closer look at the officer, the one who had a nose plate and dark glasses. He pointed his finger at me like a gun and pulled the trigger.

Moving closer to him with caution, I apologised for my actions, telling him that I could not remember anything, pleading for forgiveness.

'You pulled a good punch, mate. I didn't see that coming.' He pulled his sunnies up, both eyes black, blue, and puffy.

'Again, I'm so sorry,' I pleaded. My legs weakened.

'Well, we gave you a few souvenirs, something to remember us by.' He gave me an evil wink, smirking. He had a silver tooth.

I felt like a rhino had hit me. He gave me another smug smirk, telling me to piss off and to watch my back and that he wouldn't lay charges, just would get even someday. I vaguely remembered him from the school when Hieu went off on the shooting frenzy.

Lucy met us back at the school, we embraced until Brother John and the vice principal walked towards me with purpose. I was instructed to go to the office immediately. We nervously waited while Lucy smothered Dad in kisses and hugs. They chatted momentarily until BJ, the vice principal, and Dad met for over an hour, the most extended hour I have ever spent.

Lucy kept rambling on about the gig, music, rehearsals, and the next gig. She wouldn't be quiet. Then, finally, BJ walked out with little Chammy in tow puffing away vigorously. He went first, followed by Dad and the vice principal.

'Archie, due to the circumstances, this is your first – and last – warning. Mess up or disgrace our school's name ever again, you and your sister are out of the school and back to the farm,' BJ said.

I had never felt so ashamed. Looking at Father, words were not needed. He was clearly upset, looking drained from lack of sleep.

'You're officially on probation,' the vice principal said. 'Last chance, Archie. Here, we pride ourselves on integrity. We have no room for, and we will not tolerate disobedience of this sort. You can thank your father for allowing you to stay. We have the paperwork to send you packing. Do you understand?' He was tall, mean, grey, and bold with glasses. 'Now, to the principal's office for some corporal punishment.'

I walked up the flight of stairs. The floorboards creaked as my feet moved over the worn navy-blue carpet. I opened the door. Principal Jones stood there tapping the metre or so long thin cane up and down on his palm. Two swift whacks on my palms, it stung like hell. I figured that was it.

'Now, turn your hands over,' he demanded.

My knuckles now exposed; I saw the evil glimmer in his eye as he began to thrust the cane towards my knuckles. Instinct took over, and I pulled my hand away. The cane went smashing onto the corner of his massive wooden desk, breaking in half.

'No way, sir, no way, not on my knuckles.'

The principle furiously confronted me, over towering me. 'Put your palm out again,' he said, and I received an extra two whacks across the fingers for my troubles.

'If I ever see you in here again, Saunders, you will be sorry. Now, get out of my office!' he yelled, pointing his long, dangling, branch-like finger at the door.

Dad put his arm around me. 'What a man gotta do for his kids?' he said, walking outside and trying to give me some comfort.

All I wanted to do was tell him the news about our first live performance. At the same time, I felt proud but awful. My heart was bleeding and torn in half.

'I've heard about the gig,' he said, after what seemed an eternity of silence. 'I hear it went down well and that you practised and rehearsed with a great group of guys and formed a band and a bond. Archie, look, you are only 16. Please do not make the same mistakes I made. I get it. I understand that you want to celebrate and have a good time with your band mates, but you cannot destroy people's property. You cannot vandalise and assault people, especially police offi-cers. Seriously, what were you guys thinking? You are so lucky the constable didn't lay assault charges on you, son. Only God knows why he didn't.'

We talked and talked. It was unreal to see him again. Then, he told me a story about when he had been in a band as a lead singer around my age. When he turned 18, he had been trouble with the law. He had spent 12 months in prison. His band had signed to a record label, but due to his actions, the band's dreams destroyed.

'Crime doesn't pay,' he said. 'Do you have a girlfriend, Archie?'

'There is this one girl I like.'

'Well, when you are 18 and get on an assault charge like this, you will do a minimum of two years hard prison time, and a young, fresh, good-looking guy like you will end up being a hard criminal, maybe with a girlfriend. Forget your music career; you will not be allowed to leave the country, like me. It won't matter how successful you are. If you do time, you won't be able to tour the world with a criminal record, mate.'

He looked at me and hugged me. 'Love ya, Arch. Your mother loves you. Never forget she is always looking down on you as your guardian angel up there in Heaven, okay? Plus, you have a responsibility now. You have to look after your little sister and become a role model. I have sent you to this school with full faith and trust in you, mate. Don't let us down again. Could you not make us look like a fool?'

'I'm sorry, Dad.'

'Well, Archie, sometimes sorry means sweet bugger all, it's too late; the damage is done.

'I have to get back to some hard yakka on the farm to pay your school fees and now pay this debt back. I was young and stupid once, blew my chances and dreams, then I met your Mother. The first time I laid eyes on her at the checkout at the general store, she had the smile of an angel. She is an angel. We got married two years later. Then, she gave birth to you, then your sister. That's the best thing that has ever happened to me, you two little miracles. I have to go now,' he said. 'Let your soul get sold to rock 'n' roll, Archie. You have the talent. You have a look. You have the guts, the balls. It all means nothing if you don't have the song or synergy of a band. You're the lead singer, and you're the front man. You write the songs and melodies. You're the director of your dynasty. Take control, work hard, stay articulate. Be the best you can. Sometimes the power of music, words can say something that you can't really express. And more importantly, if I have to bail you out again, Archie Saunders, you're on your own.' Dad gave me another big hug, then jumped into his old beat-up Holden, about to drive off.

I had just spent a day and a half behind bars and been beat up. I never wanted to do that again. I didn't even get to go to the disco. What a night out.

'Hey, Dad, before you go, what did Grandpa do in the war? He told me he was a radiographer. 'I heard he was a pilot.'

Shrugging, Dad switched the engine over. 'Make sure you find a dawn service. I understand the shrine of remembrance and the march is worth a look. It's in a few weeks, April 25th. Make sure you pay your respects, okay? And stay out of trouble, will ya?' He paused, then added, 'Hey, Archie?'

'Yes, Dad?' I replied.

'A wise man once told me, it doesn't matter how good a musician you are, you have to entertain the crowd... You can be the best guitar player, but if you have no stage presence and don't entertain people, it won't matter how good you are; be an entertainer, okay?'

'Okay, Dad. I will.'

I would miss him more than I thought. I waved goodbye.

He took a sip out of his faithful coffee mug. 'Think of Elvis, Jim Morrison, Mick Jagger, Freddie Mercury, Michael Hutchence, or even Neil Diamond, Archie. They all have a huge stage presence, you understand. I loved all them acts. Mum adored Neil Diamond; she would always have his records on when cleaning or late at night when they had what they called special sleep time.'

'Okay, Dad, I'll remember that,' I said, holding onto my sore palm and swollen knuckles.

He drove off, beeping and doing a small burnout on the way out of the gravely dirt driveway. Watching and hearing his burnout made me smile.

After that, Lucy snuggled closer to me. 'I'm sure he misses us, Archie.' She gave me little whack in my ribs.

'Yeah, watch it; it hurts there.'

'Ah, you're just a big sook, Archie. Did you really punch that copper in the face?'

'Lucy, I can't remember a thing. The last thing I remember was a window smashing. I must have just snapped or something.'

'Mmm, did you know Albert Einstein didn't speak until he was four?' Lucy said.

She frequently puzzled me with things like this. It was this that made her unique. She might have been quiet and at times withdrawn, but she was extremely observant at the best and worst of times.

'No, I didn't, sis. Why you say that?'

'I dunno. I just read about it.'

'Damn, my head is banging, Lucy. I gotta get some Panadol or something.' I placed my hand on my head, trying to soothe the pain.

'I have some codeine in my room you can have. It's much better and more relaxing than Panadol.'

Lucy had her foot in two different worlds. Which one she would decide was anyone's guess.

We Roam and We Charge

Weeks passed. I borrowed a skateboard from a nearby apartment. It was the best fun, skating down Victoria Street, rushing around, dodging pedestrians and cars to catch the 57 tram into the Flinders Street for the Anzac Day ceremonies and March. The conductors or 'connies' were out in force. We cautiously dodged a fare evasion. We never paid for trams and were frequently chased by them. We knew all the back streets and alleys. A quick getaway plan was always on the cards.

Scouting around the many groups and war veterans, I was asking around about the Nhill airport when a kind man explained to me there were 35 training bases across Australia in World War II, and Nhill was one of them. He pointed me in the direction of the Royal Australian Air Force squadrons section or commonly known as RAAF.

Poking around the large crowd, I asked a few groups of people if they heard of my grandpa Richard Saunders from Netherby and Nhill.

A man with a grey beard, a walking cane with wide medal ribbons that had a wide khaki central stripe, flanked by two narrow red stripes, and with edge stripes of dark blue and light blue, responded, 'Who are you, son?'

'He's my grandpa.'

'He's your grandpa, is he?'

I nodded back apprehensively.

The man mumbled a few words to himself as the group of men were slowly getting ready to begin their march. Looking back at me, he said, 'Yes, I knew your grandfather well, son.' They started marching. 'Come on, then, son. Join us in the march.' He welcomed me into the group of a dozen or so men, all dressed in their clobber medals pinned on their chests. One man in a wheelchair seemed more interested in reading the form guide.

The crowd of onlookers clapped their hands, whistling.

'Good onya, diggers!' one man shouted.

The old man looked down at me, clearing his throat. 'Your grandpa was one of the best God damn pilots and bravest man I had the honour and privilege ever to meet.' He patted me on my back in comfort.

'Did you know him well?' I asked, as the crowd continued to celebrate, thanking the men.

'We shared a dorm in the trainees' accommodation building for a few months. Ah, yes.' He sighed. 'Right next to the parachute-drying building. I remember it like yesterday, the open ground to the left of the canteen, and we used to go to the theatre as well.

'He saved my life, son. He saved many a man's life, my boy. I wouldn't be here now if he didn't bomb the—' He paused.

'What bomb?' I asked, showing more interest.

"Dead Eye Dick" we called him,' another man joined in. 'He never missed.'

'Missed what?'

'Targets, boy. He had an excellent eye for it. He practised dropping smaller bombs for weeks at a time in the Little Desert Target Range, nurturing his skills, and didn't they come in handy?'

They all agreed in unison.

'Bloody oath,' another said.

They continued talking amongst themselves. Seven airmen lost their lives in training flights at Nhill and were buried in war graves in Nhill Cemetery. The men continued discussing, reminiscing, and sharing jokes about flying the Wirraways and Tiger Moths.

'The CAC Wirraway, which is an Aboriginal word meaning 'challenge,' was a training and general- purpose military aircraft manufactured between 1939 and 1946. It was a difficult aircraft to fly, and only the best pilots could fly them, and your grandpa was one of them son,' the man continued. 'The Lockheed Hudson was an American-built light bomber was my favourite.' He scoffed. "We roam and we charge" was the motto, son. When your pop was in the air, we knew we were in good hands.

'The military station is based at Nhill. Back in September 1941, the commanding officer was Wing Commander A.G. Carr (AFC). It was where warplanes used to train pilots in air navigation.'

'The town became a refuelling base for aircraft because of its central position between Melbourne and Adelaide,' another explained. 'The Aerodrome became a vital cog in a national network when it became host to an air radio station, providing communications and navigation support for an increasing amount of civil aircraft.'

'My pop was a worker in the station?' My eyes were wide open.

'He was a bomber, kid. Never missed. Dead Eye Dick, rest in peace, digger.' He placed his right hand across his heart. 'Courageous man he was, son, one of the best.'

I copied him, in awe. The stories these men told were fascinating while marching and waving to the thousands of people, who paid their respects.

'Bloody good cook, Ol' Dead Eye,' another joined in. 'Not sure if he's more famous for being one of the ballsiest pilots in the air or for his spag bol.'

They all chuckled together.

'Bloody good dancer, too, Old Dick,' another informed me.

Another man pulled out a hip flask from his inner jacket pocket. 'Here's to Dead Eye.' He took a healthy swig. 'That's better.' He smiled, walking tall. He gave me a nudge, handing me the flask. 'Have a swig for your old man, sonny.'

Reluctantly accepting his request, I sniffed the flask, then took a small sip. 'Yuck!' I shook my head, shivering and spitting some out. 'What's that?!'

'Mother's Milk, son.'

'Mothers Milk?'

'Rum! Your pop and I would drink gallons of this stuff. A good man, your pop, son,' he spoke with a gravelly tone. 'A tragedy about your pop and your grandma, son. You should hold your head up high. Enjoy the rest of this march.' He brushed his hands across an Australian flag held by a young family, mumbling to himself. His eyes welled up as he puffed out his chest, taking another swig. He gave me a wink, waved back to the crowd, and gave one group of people the thumbs-up.

A certain swagger, a limp. Our heroes. The old man began humming 'Waltzing Matilda'. The others followed.

'Can't wait to get back to the RSL for a few coldies,' the man in the wheelchair said, back to reading his form guide while marching. 'Flemington today, race 6. The VRC Ledgers on today. "Enchanteur" each way all day.' The man looked up towards me, grinning.

'My dad is a horse owner. He used to own The Flying Nun.'

'The Flying Nun,' he repeated. 'Ah, yes, the white horse, it won the Horsham Cup. I had a few bob on it each way, paid pretty good odds if I remember,' he said, coughing, then spluttering and giving a young family waving a small Australian flag a thumbs-up.

'Yes, she did, I was there that day,' I said happily. 'She's a Camarillo breed.'

'You know, in some cultures, white horses stand for the balance of wisdom and power. In others, like Christianity, the white horse is a symbol of death. The horse is a universal symbol of freedom without restraint, because riding a horse made people feel they could free themselves from their own bindings' he said, captivating me even more than ever.

'My horse in the war was a great war horse. A tragedy,' he said, 'it was like shooting my own son. Ah, well, good luck today, mate.' He gave me a nod of appreciation, understanding horses.

'When the chips are down, you need more than luck, son. You need a bloody good jockey,' he laughed, coughing and spluttering all over the place.

I wondered if this geezer was going to make the actual distance. 'Is he alright?' I asked another man.

'She'll be right, mate,' the man replied.

'Todays a special day, comrade. We will remember,' another said, holding his hand on his heart.

'Lest we forget,' they said as one.

'Brothers in arms,' the man in the wheelchair said.

A sense of pride and honour filled my body. I received a wry smile and wink from the man. I placed my hand across my heart, following the proud men. He took another swig and sighed. His chest puffed out; head held high. He marched, acknowledging the applause, cheers, and thank yous from the crowd. Remarkably proud.

I stood, paralysed, throughout the march, witnessing a bond between the men that was cemented in ilk. They explained the landing of Gallipoli, the war in France, Borneo, Vietnam and remembering the Battle of Crete. I never knew the suffering and the price our diggers paid for our freedom. Some of the harrowing stories I could not imagine, particularly the Battle of Crete ones that made me weak at the knees.

We roam and we charge, eh? I thought to myself. It would be a good name for a song or tattoo.

'They shall grow not old, as we that are left grow old; Age shall not weary them, nor the years condemn. At the going down of the sun and in the morning We will remember them.'

I softly spoke to myself with a grin from ear to ear. It was surreal experience; one I would never forget and respect. The whole 'she'll be right' mentality is one that stuck with me for a long time.

Holy Caspers

There are winners, and there are losers. Missing out twice in the past two years to enter the Battle of the Bands was killing us all inside. The first year was due to the Mark and Lucy incident. The second year, I ended up with influenza, couldn't sing, and barely get out of bed. It was the start 1986, the year of the tiger in the Chinese year. Our year. Summer holidays passed. We went to visit Dad at the farm, then to Uncle Charlie down in Millicent and spent some time down at Beachport. Fishing, swimming, jumping of the jetty, riding bikes in the sand dunes at Southend, playing with Rusty, hanging out, and camping sitting around the fire playing music with Dad were the best. Uncle Charlie would tell all these weird and wonderful stories about them growing up as kids. His humour was left field.

All good things come to an end, they say.

We had rehearsal. We practised and practised whenever and wherever we could. The school offered us a hall once a week, Fridays 7 p.m. to 9 p.m., after dinner before we had lights out and the church's curfew.

Live performances became scarce and limited since our debut. We'd had a handful or so live gigs that Lucy secured for us.

Lucy had pretty well given us a good case and taken over as our manager. She'd come up with our band name: The Holy Caspers. I pushed for the Seven Deadly Sins and got outvoted. That pissed me off.

She designed a logo of a cool Casper-like ghastly ghost. We arranged our set list that consisted of the likes of Rolling Stones, Led Zeppelin, AC/DC, Steve Miller Band, Hoodoo Gurus, KISS, INXS, Painters and Dockers, Bob Marley, even a Sex Pistols track to keep Gaz and Daz happy that Gazza sang. Tommy sang a few, but I sang most of them while we had a couple more original songs that Lucy and I had written that we were working on. Lucy sourced out an electronic keyboard that had loops, synthesizers, and fresh, funky sounds that Melissa learned quickly. I was teaching her how to play the guitar every now and then. Anything to be closer to her. She picked it up pretty quickly.

At one of the gigs, we had to play one song at some weird annual school showcase. No one mixed the sound, and it sounded terrible. Another was at Lucy's girlfriend's parents' house. We were shut down after three songs because of noise complaints.

We are all underage for live venues. We couldn't play in the pubs and clubs; however, at times, depending who was on the door, we would attempt our way in.

For the limited gigs done, we had a good following, so we had booked a couple of school gigs and some private parties. At one party Lucy arranged, there was a keg of beer. Everyone had to chuck in $5 to enter.

It ended with the boys in blue coming in and breaking up the party. Gazza was taken away by the police for being drunk and disorderly. Urinating on the police vehicle didn't help his case, either, not to mention vomiting in the back seat of the cop car. That's when the coppers had thrown him in the back of a divvy van, to the chorus of onlookers singing the Painters & Dockers song, 'You're Going Home in the Back of a Divvy Van', all clapping their hands to the beat, singing louder and louder, laughing.

He was held overnight, then summoned to the child's court, his second appearance in a matter of months. He was also caught doing a break-and-enter, trying to steal some alcohol and jewellery from a house in a nearby suburb. His parents, had to come into the school. The twins have been warned many times and were on a final warning. I couldn't believe they haven't been thrown out. Daz told me his parents simply give the school money and bribed them. I didn't know what to believe.

One night, we all sneaked out after our rehearsal to the local live music venue, The Bolt. Somehow, we all got away with being over 18 without checks, except my younger sister. She erupted like a firecracker when refused entrance. We all went in, telling her to go home. Thirty minutes later, I saw her entering the club. As soon as she walked into the venue and heard the live music, she moved to the groove and the beats of the electric sound while scoping out the place, similar to an over-energetic constable trying to be an undercover pimp.

I walked up and grabbed her. 'How the hell did you get into here?'

She gave me a wink and said she told them she was the manager of the band playing, and if they didn't let her in, she would never allow them to play here again. But that's what I liked about her. Considering the place was jam-packed with everyone enjoying the band, who would have guessed they'd believe that story? I didn't even believe it. The band took a break, and the DJ took over. Lucy went off to hit the dance floor in her own world of mingling and dancing away. I noticed she would begin some crazy street break dance moves, and the robot, followed by a backspin, ending up on the ground flicking her arms, legs, and twists, making the crowd cheer for more. It was pretty cool, to the track of 'Hey You' by The Rock Steady Crew. She had instant admirers and onlookers; people became magnetized to her. We could dig it as long as she kept to herself and stayed out of trouble, but sadly, trouble seemed to find Lucy.

Everybody knew it but her. She lived a haunted life. Lucy had her foot in two different worlds. Which one would she decide was anyone's guess. Only time would tell whether she could escape the past and make a new start. She became meticulous. She had many secrets, but this only furthered her despair, slipping into an inescapable form of depression overtime. If this rate continued, it would be the start of her losing her sanity.

As weeks passed, the group could feel some momentum writing and creating new songs, recording their recent creativity on an inferior quality four-track recorder. Lucy entered the room with purpose, a box under her arm, and went straight up to Leigh. She had just handed him a new eight-track recorder.

'Where the hell did you get that, Lucy?' I asked.

'I've been saving money; the boss gave me a raise' she explained defensively. I knew she had picked up some casual shifts at the local Vic markets on weekends on a fruit and veg stand, but nowhere near enough to buy one of these and Teac Tascam 8-track production system.

'Relax,' she said, 'it's secondhand.'

'It's fresh out of the box,' I said.

'Yes, but it has a small defect you can hardly see, so they gave it me a 70% discount.'

Leigh shrugged his shoulders. 'I had a good look at the system. Whoa, Lucy. It's a Teac Tascam Studio 8. I've gone through some facts and read about these bad boys. It even has a midi sequencer and synchronizer, and you can work with synthesiser's drum machines.

'Hey, I play drums. Fuck the machines,' Gazza butted in.

'Yeah, yeah,' Leigh responded, glimmering at his new toy. 'Holy shit. It even has a video and film production setup in it. We can make a bloody video clip.'

We all gathered around, amazed at the new system. It took Leigh around 30 minutes to set us up, gathering the group together for a trial.

'This will get you in that Battle of the Bloody Bands, eh?' Lucy asked.

I still wondered how she paid for this. I was scared something was not quite right.

Did she steal it, borrow it, how much a raise did the boss give her, did she lease it? What the heck?

We all got together. Three hours later, we had some sound quality recordings. Everyone was stoked with this outcome.

'Lucy, you little ripper,' Tommy said, embracing her. He gave her a big hug, then we all joined in with a group hug.

Over the past year or so, I started hanging out with different girls. Having more friends who were girls than boys, I liked it like that, though.

Melissa and Tommy were inseparable, yet in this group hug, I became aware something was different between them. I was currently seeing a girl from a school in the next suburb. We would sneak in and out of her home and school to meet in the park to fool around a bit.

She was a tall, slim blonde with long hair and blue eyes, brilliant, sophisticated. She was a year younger than me; I was nearly 17, frustratingly still a virgin. I had been steady with other girls over the period. Close, but no cigar. Deep down, I still had feelings for Melissa.

Not wanting to tread on toes, I gave up until now. Her first signal of distress nearly went unnoticed. Eyes filled with compassion;

a trickle of perspiration betrayed the tension within. She reached for my hand. I greeted her warm, soft hand.

The relationship between Melissa and me was amazing. We would often spend hours together doing homework, riding skateboards, bikes, and playing arcade games. We had an assignment for photography and spent hours experimenting with lights, background, and clothes. Melissa and I worked well together, taking a heap of photos of each other, the band and surrounding area. She looked like a model at the best of times and had a European look. She would tell me how she wanted to go to university, which I was unsure about. I just wanted to be in the band and rock.

Our spirits could not be broken.

'Stardom is anything but guaranteed,' Lucy told the group, her eyes darting all over the place, her movements erratic.

'Leigh, mix that shit up, then give it to me, and we'll send to the Battle of the Bands. Actually, make six copies for us, and I will send them to a few people as well.'

Lucy ended up sending to The Battle of Bands organizer. The biggest live music venue in Melbourne, The Espy, then to Sony Music Record Label, Mushroom, Albert Label, Warner, and hand-delivered to a local label that had just signed one of our favourite bands, INXS. The Holy Caspers was now officially out there; it was exciting times.

'This will get you in that Battle of the Bloody Bands, eh?' Lucy asked.

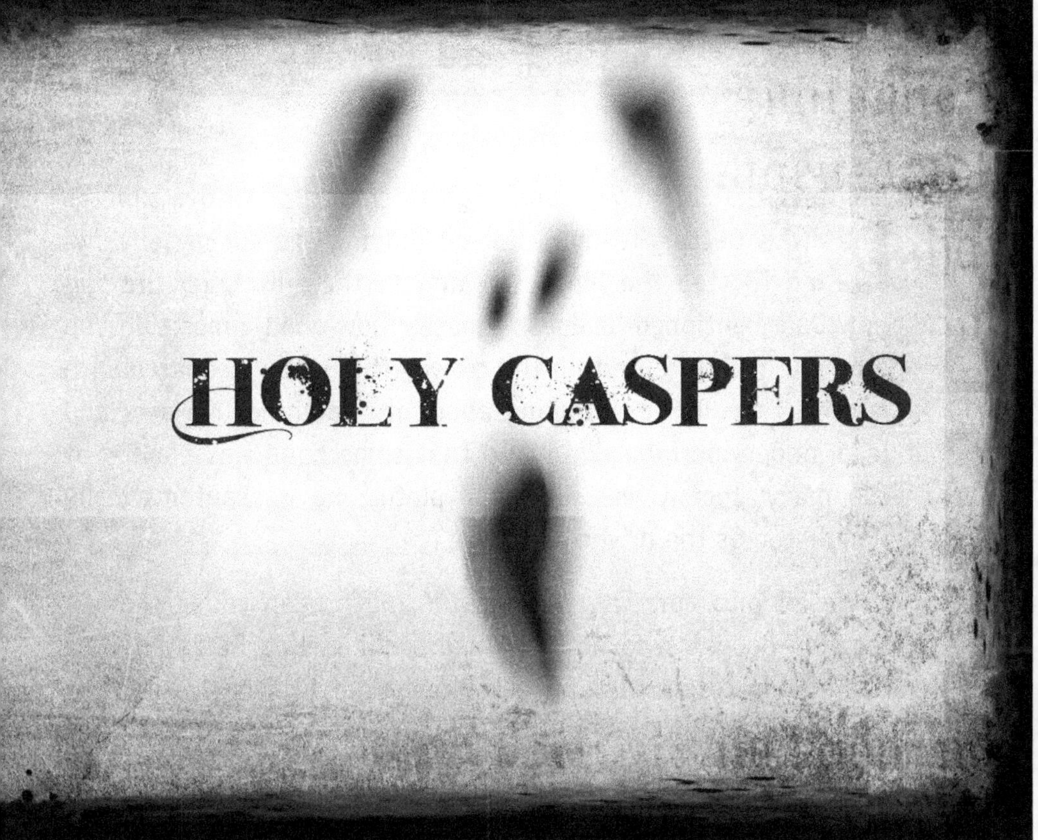
HOLY CASPERS

The Keg Party

Later that night we went to gate- crash a party five suburbs away. Getting ready, I started shaving and cut myself, trying to stop the blood, looking in the mirror, reminiscing how Dad mentioned 'It doesn't matter how good a musician you are; you have to entertain the crowd.' This really resonated with me overtime. I kept thinking about it, watching live acts and lead singers perform. We heard that some band was playing at the party. Tommy was off his P plates; he was automatically nominated as the driver.

We all piled into a 1976 Datsun 260C sedan coupe that he recently bought secondhand. I had a gut feeling Gazza and Daz had stolen it, but we never asked questions like that within this now tight-knit group.

We were all smoking, drinking, and carrying on. The volume was coming from level 13, which worried me, as I was somewhat superstitious. I never walk under ladders, avoided and hopped over cracks on the street, and never walked in front of a black cat. Didn't do reps or sets of 13 and never liked music volumes on 13. Turning the music right up, all of us sang 'Whole of the

Moon' by The Waterboys as it played on the radio. It has a little bit of everything. Brilliant lyrics, unreal drumbeat, sweet sounds of piano, great vocals, trumpet, sax solos and coolest thing of all, a comet sound effect blazing a trail! 'Woo!' Careless and free, we were all going off singing.

'With a torch in your pocket, and the wind at your heels, you climbed on the ladder, and you know how it feels, to get too high, too far, too soon. You saw the whole of the moon!'

Then... we came to some stop lights where there was a car right next to us revving his engine; this caught Tommy's eye. The cars were side by side, with the other car also filled with guys and girls; they were provoking Tommy to have a street race.

The lights turned green with Tommy accepting the challenge. The drag race was on! We sped off yelling and cheering at each other until there was another red light and had to stop. We all started to join in the prank and started to stir up the car next to us and vice versa. Green again -- we were off. Tommy was determined, he hated losing at anything and had reached up to the speed of 120 km per hour; both cars had small tyres. Tommy was behind.

I started to become anxious. The next light stayed green, with both cars flying straight through. Tommy was now on 140 km per hour, trying to catch the other car. It looked like a Toyota Corona.

'Japan piece of shit!' Tommy yelled out. His pedal was to the metal now.

'Slow down, Tommy!' I shouted at the top of my voice.

Melissa agreed and begged Tommy to slow down. Then, suddenly, the sounds of sirens and flashes of blue and red lights appeared behind us.

'Fuck me, it's the cops!' Daz yelled.

The other car slowed down, then took a sharp-left turn. Tommy slowed down to hit the brakes and took a hard-right turn, just missing another vehicle as we all squealed. My heart was racing.

'Tommy!' I yelled again as he ventured uncontrollably up the curb, just missing some pedestrians, collecting a wheelie bin along the way.

'Wheelie been over there now,' Tommy said, finding himself amusing.

Looking behind me, I spotted the police car chasing after the other car. We all took a deep breath.

Melissa blasted out at him, smacking Tommy on the arm. 'Seriously! You could have killed us, you fucking maniac.'

I had never heard her speak like that before, but she was right.

Arriving at the party, we pulled up in the garage near the keg of beer. We were gatecrashers, but Lucy knew a guy whose sister knew someone in the band or someone's boyfriend. Whatever, we just lobbed up, all half-full of beer plus bad manners, especially after the little road incident.

'Don't forget Gaz,' Daz said as he opened the boot of the car.

Gazza had been in the back while all the commotion was going on. 'What the hell happened?' he demanded.

Smoke gushed out the boot, and his brother helped him out.

As we walked through various groups, we saw a stage with a guy setting up some guitars and a drum kit, then Lucy spotted her friend. She was greeted in a way that I was not familiar with; not by a big hug, but by placing his hand on her backside, giving her a big open kiss on the mouth. It was kind of gross to watch, seeing their tongues wrapping around each other, swapping saliva and groping each other.

'Who the fuck is that?' I asked, to a shrug of shoulders. The guys were more interested in consuming and helping themselves to free beer.

'Here we go.' Leigh gestured, passing me a cup.

'Beauty,' I replied with a smile, forgetting about what we all had just witnessed. Until Lucy and her new so-called friend came over, we had been asked to pay $5 each to enter and were pointed in the direction of the keg, as well as the esky full of tallies, tall bottles of beer.

We kept close to each other, apart from Gazza and Daz, who'd smelt out the smoking areas and hung around them like bees to honey. Tommy and Melissa were in an in-depth discussion and always seemed to be arguing. Leigh and I looked at the equipment the band was using. We asked the guy a few questions about the gear, but with the reply of a few mutters, decided to hang out by the fire. The fire was in a 14-gallon drum, which kept us warm on a typical freezing-cold Melbourne night.

We were drinking the beer and checking out some of the local girls. Finishing my beer, I grabbed another from the esky and took one back to meet Leigh. I caught a glimpse of a pretty girl along the way. Thinking, *Bugger it, why not?* I stopped and said hello, introducing myself. She had a cute, round face with high cheek-bones and looked like a model. Beautiful, tall, and slim, she had black hair and a pretty smile with gorgeous snow-white teeth. We had a little idle chit-chat when I spotted Leigh looking out for me. I gave him a quick nod and asked her if she wanted to join us.

'What's your name?' I asked.

'Mary.'

'That's my mum's name,' I replied.

'Oh, okay, what does she do?'

I explained to her about Mum's accident.

'Uh-huh.'

I continued, 'Me and my sister had to move here.'

'Uh-huh,' again was the dull response.

Okay, I was thinking. There was an awkward pause. 'Would you like to join us?'

She reluctantly agreed, when a guy wearing a denim jacket his hair slicked back, bumped into me and said, 'Hey, Mary, there you are, didn't know you been mingling with some piece of scum.'

He grabbed her by the arm and pulled her away to head back inside to the party. They seemed to be bickering on the way up the stairs inside as he turned back around, sussing me out. She gave me little cute wave goodbye.

'What was that all about? She was pretty hot, though, dude,' Leigh said.

I couldn't help it, replying with now the customary 'uh-huh' and nodding.

'Yeah, well, we will never know,' I said as my eyes followed them into the room.

Gazza and Dazza were sitting around smoking whatever they could for free. Melissa and Tommy joined us after about 10 minutes or so.

So far so good, I thought, *apart from that dickhead.*

I asked if they were okay, and they both agreed they were.

'Where is your sister?' Melissa asked.

'Beats me, probably with that idiot.'

After a few beers and with no live music yet, just some crappy background music, no one was talking to us. Leaning over towards Leigh, I said, 'This joint blow's, man. The music sucks. The people are up themselves, and I've nearly been in a blew. Let's piss off.'

'I heard that he's the drummer of the band that's meant to be playing tonight,' Melissa informed me.

'Are you serious?' I had just gathered that the guy who had bumped into me and looking slick was just a dickhead, not a member of the band. Typical bloody drummers. 'Speaking of, have you seen Cheech and Chong?' I peered through the crowd.

Leigh agreed to take off; then we heard a crash, an almighty bang inside the house, followed by some howling, whistling, followed by abuse. Gazza and Daz where nowhere to be seen now.

Lucy was going off her head trying to throw punches and kicking the guy's sister.

'You try and rip me off, you little bitch!' she yelled.

The crowd of about 30 to 40 people headed towards the door. Lucy and the other girl quickly took the fight outside. I walked over through the crowd and broke up the fight when the guy who bumped into me pushed me away. Lucy, in her wild rage, brutally punched the guy fair square on the chin and knocked him out cold. Best of all, he fell back into a rose bush. There was laughter, and there were cheers, also outrage. I grabbed Lucy by the arm, heading back to the car when I saw Gaz and Dazza carrying out the keg of beer, forcing it into the back seat of the car. Running to the esky and grabbing six tallies, we all tried to pile into the car.

'Let's go, man!' Tommy yelled as he was trying to escape out of the garage.

Dazza's back door wasn't closed properly. The garage door got stuck and made a loud, destructive noise, automatically attracting some of the party-goers' attention.

'Get the fuck out of here,' Lucy demanded, squatting uncomfortably on top of the keg.

The next second, four guys checked out the car.

'We have the keg of beer in the back. I can't get in,' Lucy panicked. 'Hey, these guys are stealing our keg.'

Well, that was it; it was on like *Donkey Kong*. We managed to break free from the garage. I took a deep breath and closed my eyes until *BANG!* The keg went flying outside into the garden and rolling onto one of the guy's legs.

He screamed in pain, yelling, 'What the hell is that?'

'Everybody, pile in now!' Tommy yelled.

I ended up squeezing into the front seat with Melissa and Tommy, while the others scattered into the back, Gaz in the boot.

'Let's get the hell out of here, now!' Tommy yelled out over the top of 'Beats so Lonely' by Charlie Sexton cranking on the car stereo.

We reversed straight out the back. As we were about to take off, the car stalled from reverse into first gear. That was enough time for two of the guys to smash into the window while hurling a load of abuse at us, throwing beer bottles.

'Bugger this.' Seeing red, I opened the door hard into one of the guys.

The other backed off. I lunged at him, throwing a potent punch that landed him square on the face.

He took a swing back at me. Ducking, he shrieked in pain as he hit the tree next to us. Shaping up, we threw a few punches at each other, then I landed a robust low-left hook directly at his ribs, which made him collapse, clutching at them and groaning in pain. A guy pushed me from behind into the car. He lifted me off the ground barbarously by my hair.

I fought him with everything I had; he was as strong as an ox. Soon to be in a forceful headlock, my head being smashed into the car door. This guy was ruthless. I threw my head back at him, which smashed him fair square in the nose. Houdini-like, I escaped his grasp. Stepping back and rubbing my head, claret was seeping into my right eye.

'Don't poke the bear you, motherfucker,' I said.

Now bloodthirsty, the guy charged towards me. Standing my ground and closing my eyes, I delivered a nasty front kick that hit him directly into the solar plexus, sending him flying backward into the same tree. As he knocked his head, the guy bounced into the air. Wasting no time, I delivered him a severe right haymaker flush on his jaw, dropping him, unconscious. Surely, he would be eating soup for weeks.

In the meantime, the others in the back jumped up and took control of the handful of other party- goers. Tommy had the car fired up, demanding we all get back in and go. We all scrambled into the car, and floored it out of there.

'Everyone okay? Is everyone in?'

'Yes,' we all said instantly.

'What the fuck just happened? That was mayhem.'

We had a bit of a laugh, and everyone had their bit to say. The conversation was left, right, and centre when remembering I had successfully taken six tallies. Everyone rejoiced.

'How's Bruce Lee over there?' Leigh celebrated.

I was in a lot of pain; my knuckles had skin taken off them. I pulled out what seemed to part of a tooth. 'Brothers in arms,' I said, looking towards them in the back seat.

'Shit, yeah. Brothers in arms,' Tommy agreed.

Melissa tended to the wounds, grabbing my hand. 'Here, I will kiss it better.' She gave my bloody knuckles a little peck. 'There you go, all better, mister.'

We turned up the radio. Prince's 'Little Red Corvette' blasted out through the car's sound system. One thing was for sure; it was a crap car, but a rocking sound system.

'Let's get a yiros!' Daz yelled out.

'Yeah, nah...let's hit up Jimmy Wong's Chinese in good old Footscray,' Lucy replied, attempting an odd Asian accent.

'Shit, yeah, curry chicken,' we all agreed harmoniously.

The next morning, we had woken up having a couple of left-over tallies and were sitting around the table playing cards listening to 'Queen' on the tele for Bob Geldof's benefit concert called *Live Aid*. We were reminiscing and sharing stories of the previous night when Lucy entered the room with the guy she was with last night. We looked around at each other, a little puzzled and a tad hesitant.

'Hi, guys. Remember Joel, from the party we crashed last night?'

The killer lead break from 'We Will Rock You' soared throughout the room. We all said hi a little sheepishly, wondering if anyone else was to follow behind them.

'Crazy party,' Joel said.

Gazza leapt up. 'Hell, yeah, man, want some beer?'

He accepted the offer and explained that the band who played last night was who we had fought with. Funnily enough, as they couldn't play, the party had fizzled out as soon as the keg ran out.

I could only shake my head in disbelief at the sight of Joel drinking his very own beer - the beer that we had stolen from him. It was 'one of those had to be there moments', I guess. What a night out.

'Cheers,' we all chimed.

'Here's to the Battle of Bands,' Tommy cheered, laughing as he was making the toast. He nursed a sore head while icing a swollen right hand and turning up the TV.

Queen and Freddie Mercury had the sold-out crowd all chanting and clapping their hands in the air to Radio Gaga.

Remembering how my dad mentioned him when he drove off that day. Mesmerized, I studied his stage presence carefully. A smile appeared that would make any frowning clown happy.

Countdown

Melissa and I were in photography class in the darkroom alone together, checking out photos of each other we recently took for our assignment. The chemicals were heavy in the air.

'Check these out, Archie.' Melissa yawned, looked at her modelling photos hanging out to dry, photos of her, me, and the band.

'Wow, look at you, Melissa. You're a model. You look hot.' I gave her a little nudge. 'Wake up, will ya? We have to get these developed today.'

'Do you believe in Heaven or Hell?' she asked.

I wanted what I couldn't have. 'Both.' I smiled drawing closer to her. I was waffling on about anything. I just wanted to kiss her more than ever, but even with my foot in my mouth, words oozed out.

'Archie,' she interrupted. 'Ssshhhh, we both know now.' She looked towards the drapes to ensure they were alone. 'Archie, we don't have to tell anyone.' Her fingers brushed my face. 'You need a shave, cowboy,' she cheekily said. The silence that surrounded the room was deafening.

Waiting in the darkroom, our eyes met. Slowly leaning into each other, our lips brushed for the first time for a few seconds. We pulled away, smiling. Mel bit the bottom of her lip; she was clearly not tired anymore. In the spur of the moment we were caught up in, we embraced again for an open-mouth kiss, lasting for a minute or so. Her hands rubbing up and down my face, I struggled a little to breathe. Her tongue wildly lassoed mine deep down my throat. I placed her on the table, my body hard against hers.

'Oh, Archie,' she moaned, the tone of her voice visibly changing. Breathing hard, she gyrated up against me, wrapping her legs around my waist.

This is it, I thought. The sound of my zipper made me gasp for air, when suddenly a knock came from the door.

'Archie, Melissa, are you okay? Have the photos been developed?'

I was startled and tumbled backwards, knocking over two plastic trays with tongs in them. Quickly trying doing my fly back up, Melissa was giggling and smirking.

'Hello?' Another knock. 'Let me in.'

I opened the door.

'What's going on in here?' Mrs. Dixon, the photography teacher, asked.

Melissa was back to looking at the prints.

'These look magnificent. Look at you guys. Melissa, you are so photogenic, so sensual in this one. I love it. Where did you take these?'

'I took them in Mel's dorm and some in the studio here when we had the assignment.'

'Oh, my God. Archie, you look like Johnny Cougar or Jim Morrison in these ones. R.O.C.K 'n' the USA,' she sang to herself. 'You guys have a real eye for it. Are these the band photos?' Mrs. Dixon looked at the ones in the tray slowly developing.

The images magically appeared in front of our eyes, some in colour, some in black and white.

'Mel, you look like a European model in these. These can be straight out of a magazine. You could be a model,' the teacher said, looking at a black-and-white photo of Mel wearing dark sunglasses and a leather jacket and a leather neck choker.

'I told you so,' I said, smiling from ear to ear, still excited from our kiss.

'Okay, come on. Let's pack this up, you two, and move it outside now.'

I had a sense Mrs. Dixon knew what was going on.

We could've have mistaken for a chemistry class was on, the amount flowing in the darkroom between us. It happened quickly and unexpectedly, but I was glad it did.

Later that night, we went to see a movie starring Paul Hogan and an American actor called Linda Kozlowski.

Wow-wee, how hot is she? I was thinking. An Australian-made movie called *Crocodile Dundee* was about an outback Australian who did exist in part—the frontiersman who walked through the bush, picking up snakes and throwing them aside, calming down water buffaloes with his hand, living off the land, riding horses, chopping down trees, a simple friendly, laid-back philosophy.

'That's not a knife,' I said to myself.

Hoge's was a legend on TV - I remembered the *Paul Hogan Show* and one of his skits as Leo Wanker, not to mention the classic Australian tourism ad, 'Put a shrimp on the barbie.' He teamed up with John Cornell as screenwriter for this movie. I liked it, and I had a feeling Melissa enjoyed it as well. Took me ages to put my arm around her while watching the flick, though. It was terrific and funny, we thought. That was basically our first date.

After the movie, we landed back in Melissa's dorm. Let's just say the night progressed really well between us. We had become a lot closer since her brother Mark had been killed by a gunshot. I had become like big brother to her. Over time, I fell head over heels in love with this girl, and that night was the best I'd ever had. It was the night that I lost my virginity...if you don't count the massage that the boys had tricked me into one night. Still excited about our darkroom session, I had no clue what to do, but with Melissa's experience, she led me all the way.

'Wait here,' she said as she walked into the bathroom.

My heart was racing. Mel entered the room again, wearing red lingerie. The silhouette from her arm on the doorway, her body held the perfect curves.

She was holding a condom. 'Are you ready for this?' she asked.

I backed up onto her bed head. Sitting there merely in bland silence, I didn't expect to find what I did inside the room. Candles, rope, fluffy handcuffs, a leather whip, feathers, massage oils, and lights were dimmed.

Holy shit, I thought.

Mel was so soft and amazing, kissing, her tongue frantically circling and spiralling around mine. We were both now naked, and she was giving me instructions.

'Lower,' she said. 'Lower.'

I think I was trying to put my penis in her belly button or something.

'Ahhh, too low.' She giggled, placing her had around my erect penis, gently putting it into her moist vagina.

I was in Heaven. Like a mad rabbit, it was the best 90 seconds of my life.

Melissa wasn't as thrilled as me, though. 'Oh, Archie, that was your first time, wasn't it?'

'Yes,' I answered, now feeling a bit gawky and embarrassed.

She ignited a joint. 'Here, have some of this and relax.' Taking a few puffs, Mel moved toward her tape recorder. In the background, Lionell Ritchie's song, 'Say You, Say Me' was on. That set the scene. 'Come here, you.' She snuggled up to me in bed, rubbing her body over me.

I've been waiting for this moment all my life, I thought, finally feeling free.

Every night we slipped into bed with each other after dinner, by sneaking back to our dorm. Rain, hail, or storm, no matter what, we became inseparable. Sooner or later, learning that 90 seconds in the sack was not much enjoyment for Mel, I had to take it slower, prolonging the time. Mel gave me oral, massages, kisses, cuddles, and love; she had all the utensils and toys. She blew my mind. Mel was my first true love.

Miss Cummins, the advanced English teacher, called out my name, but I was daydreaming. A scrunched-up paper hit me in the back of the head.

'Archie, what are you daydreaming about?' she asked.

The class laughed.

'I want to be an entertainer,' I said, greeted with the sniggers and giggles in the room.

'You're dreaming of being an entertainer,' the teachers replied, seeming interested.

'Yes, Miss Cummins,' I replied, turning back to spot the culprit who threw the paper. 'A rock star, just like my dad.' I liked this English teacher much better than Mrs. Reeves. Miss Cummins talked at me, not to me or down to me, plus she was younger and cuter. I think I had a small crush on her.

'Archie?'

'Yes, Miss?'

'If you found out that you had only one more night to live... would you be happy and satisfied with what you have achieved so far, or would you give up on your dreams, or fight, chase, and hold onto those dreams?'

'I would fight, Miss Cummins.'

'The struggle to chase your dreams. The struggle to never give up on your dreams.' She stepped away from her desk. 'Never stop dreaming. Wake up and chase your dreams.' The teacher began to slowly walk around the room addressing the students.

'What do you have to lose? Don't just dream when you're asleep; dream when you're alive as well. Chase your dreams and your nightmares will grow tired of chasing you. Don't chase your tail; chase the thing makes you feel excited and gives you hope and will make you become a better person.' Her voice heightened. She steered towards me smiling.

'Everyone has a 2000-word assignment to complete. It's up to you what you want to write about. It's okay to dream, if you want to write more than 2000 words, you go for it ok Archie'. Her smile warmed my cockles.

Onwards and upwards, we wanted to win the Battle of the Bands. This year's prize was bigger than ever, a spot at the local music festival.

We had to beat the bands from the other schools. This was the Battle of Bands.

It was time to practice leaps and bounds. We rehearsed every day. This was our third — and our last — chance, to win it. Last year I came down with a virus and picked up influenza and couldn't sing the year before when all the stuff went down with Mark and Hiue.

The band was really tight, in a good headspace. Footy had finished; Tommy had won Best and Fairest for the second year in a row and had footy scouts looking at him. Gazza and Dazza stopped playing cricket. We would all go to the MCG to watch a one-day game, joining the crew at Bay 13. The best was when the West Indies was touring. We sang the theme song, 'Come on, Aussie, Come On, Come On, Come On, Aussie, Come On'. It was awesome fun at the cricket, especially during the Benson and Hedges World Cup Series, playing against England in the first final. It was a rain-reduced game. Legend Dean Jones scored a slashing 67; we loved smashing the whining poms.

We jammed and rehearsed in our spare time as much as we could. Lucy submitted our songs - and we were selected to perform at the Battle of the Bands - finally. We all knew this was our lucky break. Seven bands with only one winner.

The winner would perform at the local music festival and win a recording deal. We had to beat the band called The Court Jesters. We had been in altercations with them a few times. We hated them, and they hated us. We didn't know until now that they were the guys who started the fight at the keg party we crashed and had the tags TCJ all over our territory.

This year, the festival headliner was INXS, still having success releasing hit after hit. INXS had just released a new album called *Listen Like Thieves*.

We all respected their music and work ethic and listened to their records.

We enjoyed heaps of Aussie acts: The Angels, Divinyls, AC/DC, Nick Barker and the Reptiles, Cold Chisel, The Church, Sunny Boys, Radio Birdman, Boys Next Door, The Chain, Hoodoo Gurus, Painters and Dockers, the list goes on. We watched *Countdown* religiously every Sunday night, no pun intended. That was our dream: to play live on *Countdown*. So many success stories from the emergence of Sherbet's supposed rivals, Skyhooks, coincided almost precisely with the advent of *Countdown*, the band that was booed off at Sunbury in January '74 where Dad was working as a roadie. Dad would tell me lots of stories about how the Aussie pop scene was on fire by the mid-'70s and how Skyhooks was creating records with their debut album, *Living in the Seventies*.

Accomplishing box office success saved their label from extinction, establishing Mushroom as an influential new player in the Australian record industry. Skyhooks was the first group to appear on the first colour edition of the show in March 1975.

Their cult following gained by being the first artists played on the air when the ABC launched *Double Jay* in January that year, like a rocket launched into massive mainstream success. In no uncertain terms, *Countdown* was pivotal for both Skyhooks and their label. The owner had been struggling against very unfavourable circumstances to get airplay for artists on his roster, but when *Countdown* arrived, he hit upon the opportunity to avoid the grip of commercial radio. Exploiting this opportunity to the maximum extent possible and *Countdown* was happy to help out. So, that was what we all wanted to do as well: Follow those footsteps to perform live on *Countdown*.

Other significant beneficiaries of *Countdown*'s patronage were the Alberts Stable: Cheetah, Stevie Wright, John Paul Young, The Angels, Rose Tattoo, William Shakespeare, Flash & The Pan, and TMG. Above all, *Countdown* almost single-handedly broke AC/DC into the Australian music market. Most of the band's new clips were explicitly made for *Countdown*; 'Jailbreak' was one of the first clips to incorporate movie-style sound effects, and their legendary 'It's a Long Way to the Top' clip was shot especially for them in Melbourne by the *Countdown* crew.

AC/DC's live performance was of Bon Scott dressed as a schoolgirl and Angus Young as schoolboy, blasting out 'Baby, Please Don't Go'. It's crazy, but Bon was way ahead of his time.

Pseudo Echo had their Big break on *Countdown* with 'You're Not Listening'. This was our same goal. I mean, who wouldn't want to be interviewed by Molly and also Gavin Wood? They had so much enthusiasm for music.

Countdown launched and supported a vast range of Australian acts so far: Australian Crawl, The Church, Eurogliders, Richard Clapton, Jo Jo Zep & The Falcons, Paul Kelly, The Saints, Split Enz, who also formed Crowded House, Moving Pictures, Uncanny X-Men, Mental as Anything, Men at Work, Little River Band or LRB, Flowers (who changed their name to Icehouse), Pseudo Echo, Andy Gibb, The Swingers, The Reels, Models, Kids in the Kitchen, The Radiators, Wa Wa Nee, Sharon O'Neill, the band I'm Talking with singer Kate Ceberano, who I had the hots for when growing up and had the TV week poster on my wall. All these acts owed an enormous debt to *Countdown*.

International acts like Wham, Madonna, and R & B influenced J Geils' band's song called 'Centrefold'. Billy Idol, Blondie, Wham, David Bowie, Elton John, and Molly's interview with Prince Charles, Molly's famous catch cry to promote an album: 'Do yourself a favour'. Why not discover our band, The Holy Caspers with 'Carefully Sold', to give us some national exposure?' One of my dreams of releasing a remake of 'Locomotion' had already been dashed though, when a TV soapie called Kylie beat me to the mark of releasing the song.

ABBA was also unearthed to the nation and became an international success thanks to *Countdown*. I had the hots for the blondie, Agnetha. And how saucy was Samantha Fox! I had a poster of her up on my wall; so many great acts, I could go on and on! Dad knew a few of them while touring in his band and working as a roadie; sometimes a few of his bandmates would stay at the farm and play music.

Countdown became a hit maker, with acts as Sherbet and Daryl Braithwaite's solo career. The Easy Beats, Stevie Wright, John Paul Young, Marcia Hines, Vanda and Young, including the international acts and interviews with Elton John and Bay City Rollers while Glam Rock was introduced to our TVs and shores from Hush, The Sweet, and many more. It was an era of young girls clutching at artists' groins, a revolution within the producers of the ABC, experimenting with the latest technology, and any unknown act would leave as a mega-star. Even the Wombles had a cameo on *Countdown*. We had to perform on this TV show.

The Vapours' hit, 'Turning Japanese', plus the Split Enz song, 'I Got You', was a massive hit and stayed at number one for eight weeks, which replaced Queen's 'Crazy Little Thing Called Love' that had seven weeks at number one. Neil Finn wrote the song; the video clip was outrageous, with him singing in a room and the band behind him in picture frames, animating when he hit the chorus. It was wild.

Seriously, who could forget the live performance of Cold Chisel on *Countdown* in '81, smashing up the stage, Jimmy Barnes saluting the crowd with a bottle of vodka, Mossy smashing his guitar into the amps, the band uniting, sticking it up the industry? TV Week was awesome. 'Eat this,' Jimmy finished with. They cleaned up the awards that year, and they never gave a rat's yahoo; how cool. *Countdown* also brought fashion into the limelight, which Lucy loved, and the music was its mentor; it was a genuinely creative and essential period for music, video, and presentation.

Gaz and Dazza got into their punk-rock bands: The Hard-Ons, The Saints, Nick Cave, and especially The Painters and Dockers, which had a heavy influence on their musical style, but rarely made it on *Countdown* to perform, if ever. Tommy and Leigh had American influences such as Van Halen, Motley Crew, Judas Priest, Def Leppard, Led Zep, Jimmy Hendrix, Cheap Trick and Aerosmith. They had most of their records as well and introduced me to an album called *Appetite for Destruction* from a new band called Guns & Roses, or abbreviated as GNR, that I really liked. The guitarist of GNR, Slash, really rocked.

Sitting around Gaz and Dazza's room, the twins wore their customary white bonds' singlets, bickering, playing cards and Yahtzee. I smoked away, flicking through a gossip magazine. The front page exploited Lady Diana, Princess of Wales, and made me feel ill. I loved Princess Diana, having cut-out photos of her on my schoolbooks and diary. After she became the Princess of Wales, Diana automatically acquired rank as the third-highest female in the United Kingdom order of precedence after the Queen and the Queen Mother. Lady Diana first met Prince Charles, the Queen's eldest son and heir apparent when she was 16, in November 1977, dating her older sister, Lady Sara. The paparazzi swarmed upon her and her children like stricken poison ivy, especially while on their holidays.

I sat in Gaz and Dazza's room, stressed out that my advanced English teacher, Miss Cummins, had given me a massive assignment, a 2000-word story. I had to pass year twelve. Melissa kept talking about going to university and pushed me to study hard and get my grades up, which Dad was happy about. However, I had a few ideas. I was thinking, maybe a story on how I ended up at this school and writing some songs and forming a band. I couldn't think straight and wanted to write about a drug-fuelled youthful defiance. It was impossible, yet all true, though. Or about a grieving family who struggled to make peace with the untimely event of their mother's death.

Two sides of the coin to choose from. It was hard to decide. *Make your mind up*, my brain combusted. *Choose one.* I was getting weary thinking about it, daydreaming again, flicking my new lucky Zippo on and off, having a whirlwind of distractions. Confused and stoned, I turned towards the gang blankly and put my notepad and pencil down. I clearly had no inspiration and was easily distracted. Melissa put The Beatles' 'Lucy's in the Sky with Diamonds' on the record player. 'I love this song,' she said, tinkering around on her new Korg keyboard. 'Turn it down for a sec, Archie,' she said, motioning towards the record player.

'Where's Lucy?' Gaz asked.

'Dunno.' I shrugged, puffing on a spliff while Gaz and Daz were playing Yahtzee and betting on some dice game.

Melissa was playing some nice music.

'What's that?' I asked.

'Just making it up. This new keyboard has some fresh sounds.'

I listened attentively. 'That's nice, Mel.' I blew smoke in her direction.

'Pass that over' she said. 'Lucy's in the sky, na, na, da, da,' she softly sang, playing the chords of C and F.

'Sing that again,' I said.

'Say what?'

'Sing that again, Mel,' I requested.

She tinkered away again with the intro of 'Lucy's in the Sky', then looked directly at me, taking a puff of the joint, smiled, and followed with, 'While you're so high.'

'That's catchy.' I picked up my black Yamaha 12-string acoustic guitar, strumming the same keys of C and F. 'Start again, Mel.'

'Yahtzee!' Gaz rejoiced in the background.

'Shut up, Gaz,' I said.

'Fuck off,' he snapped back, taking a drag of a Winnie Blue. 'Anyhow, have a Winfield,' he said, blowing some near-perfect smoke rings while speaking.

'Mel, again! Lucy's in the sky while you're so high.' I chimed in the next line with, 'She took a bad trip, and that was it.' The sounds of dice rolling in the background caught my attention.

'Like a roll of the dice.' There was a pause when Daz joined in, 'She sacrificed.'

Mel bounced back in, looking at me, singing, 'Her love for me.'

Strumming away, still in the chords of C and F, I sang, 'It seems like an impossible dream.' Another pause. 'Childhood memories, childhood memories.'

In sync, we moved to the key of G. 'Of the places that we have been...' We dropped it back to F, singing, '...and the faces that we have seen, together.' We were back strumming C and F. We stopped.

'That's fuckin' cool!' Gazza yelled out, rolling the dice again.

'Yeah, solid, bro,' we unanimously agreed.

Tommy casually swaggered in, with his charismatic smile lighting up the room, grasping onto half a bottle of bourbon. 'What's happening, you cats?' He was casing the place.

We all looked at each other. Mel continued playing the chords.

'Magic, Tommy, magic,' I said, strumming away. 'Could you do it again, Mel?' I asked quickly, while writing some lyrics and chords down in my trusty note pad.

We continued to jam for a little longer, then rushed to the band room to record our new song. It took us less than an hour. It was epic!

Maybe these are the moments. We've come so far, I thought. We all had come so far with our own personalities, traits, and opinions about life, and especially music. Changes occurred often with everyone's day-to-day business. What hadn't changed was the hope and the will to win the Battle of the Bands competition this time.

T C J
80'S
Style

Battle of the Bands

The Battle of the Bands was held at our local venue. It had the capacity to hold 900 people and had a kick-ass PA system.

All the Aussie touring bands played there. It was really cool.

We'd heard our name on the radio; we'd seen our name in the press and on posters around the area.

We had one chance to save ourselves from our sanity. Our third and final attempt. We all had been asking venue managers and band bookers to play in this venue for nearly two years. We were refused every time due to our age, and being at Catholic school had a so-called stigma attached to it. Little did they know we weren't all good Catholic boys and girls and weren't very religious.

Gearing myself up to finally perform at the Battle of Bands, I was listening to U2's new album, *The Joshua Tree*, 'Streets Have No Name' blasting on my new Sony Walkman that Lucy had given me for my seventeenth birthday. Bono was one of my favourite singers with his electric voice, and 'The Edge' on guitar one of my favourite guitarists as well.

The bouncers and security always watched us like hawks. They thought we were all little criminals or something. We were gathering the reputation as ones. Like the Beastie Boys, we had to fight for our right to party. We had all been kicked out of the venue over time, apart from Lucy. They all loved Lucy! I noticed her with one of them down the nearby alley arguing. I went to intervene when they spotted me. The security guy quickly ushered her back into the venue via the back door, which was slammed shut abruptly in front of me. I noticed nearby an array of used syringes scattered all over the curb and alleyway; a couple of guys squatting on the ground closely to each other spooked me.

The local radio stations and street press all supported the Battle of the Bands. We heard our name on the radio, and we'd seen our name in the stress press and posters around the area. It was cool until we saw on several posters that someone had tagged over our name. This really pissed us off; I suspected it was The Court Jesters. But as long as we beat them in the battle, I'd be more than happy.

We could make it all wrong or make it all right for tonight's Battle of the Bands. The time to play came. We were the second-to-last band to play, followed by The Court Jesters. Our band was already niggling with The Court Jesters, pushing and shoving in the green room over the posters and the party we had crashed. Luckily, the free booze was starting to run dry.

There was some white powder on the table next to a disgustingly filled ashtray. Gazza popped his head around, smiling, rolling up a five-dollar note. Sniffing the substance up instantly like a Hoover vacuum, the white powder disappeared up his nostril. 'Here you go,' he said as he handed me the rolled-up note. 'Have a go.'

'What is it?' I asked inquisitively.

'God knows, but we'll soon find out.'

Bugger it, I thought, carefully rubbing some on my tongue first, before deciding to copy Gazza. It tasted like diesel and made my mouth all numb, burning my nostrils as well.

'There you go,' said Gazza, patting me on the back. 'We're gonna rock tonight, mate.'

The crowd was fully charged up and well on their way! We headed towards the stage as one.

Lucy came racing up towards me, barking some mundane instructions.

'Have you seen Melissa?' I asked.

'Yeah, nah,' she replied, unable to stand still. Underneath the surface, something was wrong.

'So, how you doing?' I asked.

'I'm fine,' she said. 'What about you? Are things good between you and Mel?'

'Yeah, they're great.'

'That's good, Archie. I've come to like her now.'

'Finally,' I said. 'She's just a bit unusual, that's all.' I laughed and fidgeted.

'Come on, bro. There they are. Let's go.'

The moment was ours. The raw truth, drawing for inspiration, armed with the knowledge earned through years of hardship. Memories and emotions flooded my body like a raging river: thoughts of Hieu shooting Mark, being arrested, working in the fish 'n' chips shop, all the setbacks, the good times, the bad times, Rusty my dog, my dad, and most of all, my mum. It was an overwhelming feeling. Looking over at Tommy, there was something in his movement that sent alarm bells off. He wasn't himself, even his usual charismatic charm was flat as a tyre. He put his fist out, which I greeted with an almighty powerful fist pump.

'Let's do this, Tommy,' I said, trying to pump him up.

'Come on, Tommy. Brothers in arms,' Daz said, slapping him on his back, raising his beer. 'Cheers, big ears,' he added, smiling bright, taking a glimpse of himself in a reflection of a window, stopping to check out his biceps popping from his white bonds singlet top.

Tommy seemed to be suffering in self-doubt and a lack of confidence that would resound and echo with teenagers. He wasn't himself.

'I'm not sure I can do this, Arch,'

'He is a man of little faith,' Gaz arced up, also stopping to check himself out, he and his brother pretending to shape up to each other.

'She'll be right, mate,' I added, trying to comfort him.

He was quiet and withdrawn.

'Yeah, carn, man. You're killing the vibe bro,' Daz said, putting his two bits' worth in, adjusting his hair that his brother put of place.

It came as no surprise when Gaz said, 'Here, have some of this.' He brought out a small bag, placing white powder on his wrist.

'Yeah, nah, it's okay. She'll be right.'

'Suit yourself.' The white powdery substance disappeared in a millisecond up Gaz's nostril.

'Where did you get that from?' I asked.

'Nunya', he said.

'Nunya, who?'

'Nunya bloody business, cowboy.' He laughed, giving his brother another taste.

Tommy's and my eyes were transfixed, waiting and waiting, anticipating, uncertain in the suspense of this outcome making us feel like on tenterhooks. We had been through thick and thin, me and Tommy. One boozy night, we became blood brothers, slicing our palms with a small pocket knife he carried around. I think it was the same one he waved at us the first time we met. It was all the better that he was okay with me and Melissa. Tommy never had problems with girls.

Amongst the terror upon entering the stage, we kept our heads held high. Silence was followed by murmurs from the crowd. We all had a sense of *This is it...*

My eyes closed, and taking a massive deep breath, I said, 'I can do this. I can do this.' I kept repeating and thinking the mantra to myself. An unnatural feeling of power washed over me. *Man, I feel good. What was that stuff we just had?* My heart was now racing while feeling eight-foot tall and bulletproof.

Everyone had four songs they could play, so we had to choose the best of what we'd rehearsed. Turning to face the guys, I strummed the chords of G and C on my trusty old Yamaha acoustic with my sound check of 'Quo, quo, alright-yo.' I kept repeating it, blasting through the PA system. 'Quokka,' I followed with, now just messing around with the sound and ensuring the fold backs were good. I gave Leigh a wink while he frantically tried to figure out what he was doing with the massive sound-and-light system the venue had provided.

Looking up towards me, he nodded and gave me the thumbs-up while turning up the foldbacks. I was happy now and feeling on top of the world.

'Let's hit the pedal to the metal,' Daz said with his cheesy grin.

Tommy began his thing on lead guitar. Daz followed with bass. 'The Animal,' Gazza, slowly tapped away at drums, which was soon followed by Melissa on the keyboards.

Head down and bum up, our set list began with The Boys Next Door, who changed their name to The Birthday Party, classic hit, 'Shivers'.

'I've been complicating suicide.' The 900-plus crowd knew every lyric and joined in. A classic, the group began to sing to the chorus: 'Down my spine,' making the crowd participate, singing the chorus as loud as they could. We interacted with them while in unison they sang. It was something special. Looking towards The Animal on drums, Gaz was smashing them as hard as he could while his twin brother stood firmly by, thumping out big, chunky bass riffs and rocking out. The rumble of thunder discharged through out the venue, instantaneously heating up an immediate atmosphere.

We finished that song, going off as hard as we could. Tommy let loose with the start of 'Rock 'n' Roll' by Led Zeppelin. We were smashing it; the guys' harmonies were bang on. The crowd loved it, hands in the air, dancing, yelling, singing, whistling. It was super cool. I was caught up in the moment, singing, playing the harp, and busting some moves. When I looked at the mosh pit in front of the stage, it bought a sense of relief and a smile. The rumble of the crowd was electrifying; we wrapped the song up to a lion-like roar of the crowd. The adrenaline was sending shivers down my spine.

Two cute girls were smiling at me from the front row, which captured my attention. One looked familiar, and then her friend flashed her boobs. Both were giggling and smoking on what I gathered was a joint, blowing smoke up onto the stage. They were seductively licking their lips and embracing each other, luring me with their eyes while touching and stroking each other.

'Archie!' one yelled.

I was wondering who this girl was, and then it dawned on me: the 'uh-huh' girl, Mary. She was looking like Elle Macpherson, as hot as! It was on for young and old; we had stage divers, stage crashes, and a mosh pit at the front of the stage.

'We are the HOLY CASPERS! This is an original song called "Carefully Sold", I yelled into the microphone and was greeted by an enormous applause of the packed house. I looked back to the two cute girls smiling at me, who continued expressing or suggesting physical, especially sexual, pleasure or satisfaction towards me.

The intro began perfectly, then we ripped into my song. I smiled from ear to ear; it was fucking awesome!

'The sun is out. It's a beautiful day. Just sitting inside, just smoking away. Fulfilment is easy, so eager and bold.

Her mind's ecstatic. She's carefully sold. She's got a groovy feeling inside her brain.

She might be crazy; she might be insane.

She's gonna leave it up to you to see what she can do. So, let's hang out. Just let it go.

Just loosen up coz it's time to go.

It's time to go, ohh. I don't know where coz, actually, honey,

She just doesn't even fucken care. She's sold; she's bold.

She's CAREFULLY SOLD!'

Singing and pouring my heart out, I ripped out my harmonica. I tore out, up a solo break, collapsing on the ground and spinning around on my back. I felt the girls grab my feet, spinning me like a turtle in its back, running their hands all over my legs and stomach.

'Hey, Archie,' Mary said again, rubbing my groin.

The two girls were giggling as I noticed Melissa giving me a greasy look.

I could lip-read, 'What the fuck, Archie!'

Midway through the song, Tommy was pulled off the stage by his legs by a group of girls on the other side.

Amazingly, he kept on playing, not missing a beat. Before I knew it, I could see him crowd-surfing, still playing the guitar, legs swirling around like a two-legged octopus.

It was simply insane. We wrapped up the song and had to stop completely. Tommy was stuck in the crowd.

Glaring through the lights, I could see Tommy, and then he wasn't there. There was a large 'oohhh' followed by some screams of terror from the crowd. Tommy had landed heavily on his back and winded himself, dislocating his elbow.

Leigh spotted him by shining the lights into the crowd. Everyone nearby had formed a circle around him. He was in a world of pain, grimacing and clutching onto his elbow. Tommy made his way through the crowd, security helping him back onto the stage. His elbow was one way and his forearm the other. It looked terribly painful.

Announcing into the microphone, one of the security men asked, 'Is there a doctor in the house?'

'Is there a dog in the house?' Gaz thumped on his drums, singing.

Daz chimed in, thundering bass riffs in the background.

The odds were on our side. A young medical student, who was in the crowd, forced his way through the hot and sweaty crowd. He jumped up on stage, embracing Tommy and mucking around with this new song.

'There's a dog in the house.' We messed around, jamming for a minute or so.

A few words were spoken between the two. Then, out of the blue came an unholy snap, followed by a yell of pain that wallowed over the microphone.

'Ohhhh,' the crowd murmured.

'I got it!' the student yelled in joy. 'I can't believe it. I got it.'

The crowd erupted in joy. The charming young student hurled himself back into the crowd, surfing, saluting, and smiling. Tommy gave him the thumbs-up to say 'Thanks, mate.'

Shaking my head, I turned to Gaz and Dazza in disbelief.

Tommy picked up his guitar, quickly retuned, gave me a nod, and said, 'She'll be right, mate. Let's go.'

I wasn't sure what to do - or if I would vomit. I had just seen an arm snapped back into place by the student who did a stage dive and disappeared into the crowd. It was time to put the pedal to the metal for our next song, 'I want you, to want me' by Cheap Trick. Watching the young doctor move through the crowd until he disappeared through the cracks was like magic. I remembered what Dad said. *It doesn't matter how good a musician you are; you have to entertain the crowd... You can be the best guitar player, but if you have no stage presence and can't entertain people, it won't matter how good you are... Be an entertainer.*

Climbing up on the speaker, I howled a quick bluesy harp solo. The speaker was rocking side to side. I had the crowd in the palm of my hands. We started the second verse, then I had everyone singing the chorus. Tommy ripped into the lead break, head banging, wobbling side to side. Sitting on the speaker, I looked down, smiling at the two girls and singing my lungs out to the jam-packed crowd.

'I want you to want me. Feelin' all alone without a friend, you know you feel like dyin'. Oh, didn't I, didn't I, didn't I see you cryin'?' I sang, getting everyone to clap their hands.

I turned back towards Melissa for her keyboard solo, who was just shaking her head as she witnessed me flirting with the two girls, then *BANG!*

That was the last thing I remember of that night. Some yobbo threw a full can of beer, scored me straight in the sweet spot, and knocked me out. Falling from the top of the eight-foot speakers, I landed face-first off the stage, smashing on the floor in front onto the two girls. I crashed on broken beer bottles, slicing my arm and back like barbed wire.

Battle of Bands

The Break or End

I ended up in the hospital.

I woke up alone pretty well, freaking out and in a world of pain. What happened at the gig, what happened to me, what day was it, where was I? It felt like a dream. I reached for the buzzer. A male nurse walked in. My neck was in a brace, head bandaged. My right arm and back had a total of 88 stiches, and all wrapped up, my right leg was in plaster, elevated. I was busted up.

'Hello, Mr. Saunders. How's your head? You've been out for four hours. Your friends are a lively bunch, aren't they?' he said with a cheeky smile, explaining briefly what happened and where I was.

Suddenly, Lucy charged into the room.

'Holy crap, Arch, are you okay? That was wild. A beer can smashed you, knocking you out cold. The guys ended up having to cut it short and finish the song. Tommy had his elbow dislocated. It was one wild gig, bro. Gaz and Dazza found the guys who threw the can at you and then smashed them really bad. It was the guys from The Court Jesters, the bloody assholes. Leigh spotted them in the crowd and shone lights on them. Security threw them out; they couldn't perform, the suckers.'

'Did we win?' I asked gingerly. 'Did we win?'

Lucy responded, 'We are supporting INX-fucking-S. The manager was in the crowd, and, well,' she paused, 'he was pretty well horrified and stunned. I bumped into him on the way out, so I said hi. He replied, then I approached him, explained who I was, and wham, bam, thank you, ma'am, he gave me his number. He wants us to support the up-and-coming Australian INXS tour, Archie.

'You guys are bloody crazy. We bloody well won, Archie. We didn't finish the set, but we bloody well won. How's that make you feel, brother?'

I recall just smiling.

'It gets so much better, bro. Molly bloody Meldrum was there. I introduced myself, telling him I'm the band's manager, and he loved us. He wants us to perform live on *Countdown* in two weeks. It's going to happen, Archie. You've done it. He sends his regards, actually. Such a nice bloke.'

'In two weeks,' I said, evaluating my injuries. I was doubtful. 'How?' I asked with a trembling voice.

She slowly shook her head. 'I know you're down and out, bro. It doesn't matter. We can make it, and we should take it. You can count on me, so don't be so hard on yourself, mate. She'll be right.'

'You're my hero, Archie,' Lucy said as I lay there motionless.

My bright eyes searched upwards in the darkness, and I grabbed Lucy by the arm, spotting what looked like fresh rope burns around her wrists, along with a small tattoo of a musical semi-clef on the back of her neck.

She rubbed at her wrist. 'Don't worry about that.' She pulled her hand away, motioning towards the end of her neck. 'I just got a tattoo. It's cool, eh?'

I wanted to find the truth in this web of lies.

'Lucy, I want to know how you made that money, and why you kept seeing Brother Emmanuel.'

She sat down next to me and began to fill me in.

'Well, firstly, I was merely on the hunt for a buck.'

'Umm, okay,' I said.

'Remember that strip where that woman said hi to you on our first night?'

'Yes, of course.'

'Well, I used to go there. You know, hang out, and one night The Creep pulled up. I didn't recognise him. He didn't detect who I was. He paid for some attention, Archie. After a few nights doing this, we figured out who we were.'

'Paid for some attention. What's going on, Lucy?' I was starting to panic.

'Calm down, brother. Don't get your panties in a knot. Cut it out, okay?' She smiled, her eyes darting around and casing out the room. 'Then, one day at school, I decided to go to the confession box and, you know, like you said the first day, we went there and cleansed my soul and asked for forgiveness of my sins. The Creep was in the confession box, summoned me to his dorm, and showed me some photos of me working, hopping in and out of cars, in and out of clubs on that strip. He blackmailed me. He forced me to have sex with him and other students while he watched. He supplied me with grass and made me sell it to other students and people on the strip and clubs. He was going to kick us out of school, Archie, so I just went with it. However, he will pay, no doubt about that. I have made some good and bad friends over the years. He will pay.'

I listened to her story, trying to take it all in, but didn't know what to say.

'Remember the copper whose nose you broke that night out, and he was at school of the day when Hieu went ape shit?' she continued. 'He was there helping on the case. Well, let's say I got to know him, and that's why he never laid assault charges on you to start with, plus doing some business with a few of his friends who are now detectives. And my boyfriend is the young bouncer at The Bolt.' She winked. 'I don't know for sure, but I bet my dog on it that *He will get his*! We set up a honey trap for him.'

Lucy pondered and gazed out towards the sky, likely having thoughts of The Creep tying her hands up, molesting her for the first time, working on the streets, the bouncers touching her up, when deals went wrong, police enforcing her to do bad things to get me off the hook, her Italian boss in the fruit and veg stall at the Vic Markets and the 'jobs he made her do'... She turned back to me. 'He's fucked. They're all fucked and will get theirs, Archie.'

'Wait, what do you mean, Lucy, business?' I shrugged. It was a mystery to me.

'There is a spotlight that needs to be shone on the situation of lay abusers because there is much darkness there,' she said, sniffling and wiping her nose.

It was clear to me. Her instability was plain.

'Whether you're in the church pew, in the sacristy, or on the blacktop on the playground, it is the same vibe,' she added. 'Whether it's the principal, the athletic director, or the janitor, it is the same thing. Whatever power a child can have is stolen from them.'

I couldn't believe my ears or eyes.

'It's him outside my dorm. He's the rustling of twigs. The shadows. He has been watching me in bed?' I knew it wasn't the dog. I grabbed her wrist again. Were these rope marks questioning her? I remembered seeing ropes in The Creep's dorm. 'It was The Creep who did all that graffiti on the walls, isn't it, Lucy?'

'Hey, Archie,' Lucy butted in. 'Don't worry about it. I'm a big girl now.'

'You're only 16 years old!'

She piped back at me, 'Yeah, well, guess what? You made it. *Countdown*, they want you to perform "Carefully Sold" on *Count*-bloody-*down*.'

'What about the money, the drugs and selling?' I asked.

'Well...' There was a pause. '...yes.' She scanned the room, came closer to my ear, then whispered, 'I held up some chemists and stole some prescribed drugs. Ran in, ran out, had a replica gun, scared the hell out of the person at the counter. What many people don't understand is just how many drugs are perfectly legal and obtainable over the counter that are far stronger and more dangerous than illegal ones.'

'You're shitting me, right? What do you mean you held up chemists?'

'Well, diethyl ether or ether is the street name. Codeine is widespread and easy to access. Morphine you name it. I gave whatever I stole to the guys who worked at the clubs. They make up some form of pill, powder, or crystal and then sell into the clubs, on the streets, wherever. We're making a killing, mate, just like your song, "Carefully Sold". She laughed.

Is she high now? I wondered, the penny had dropped why she had codeine in her room that day.

'Even them coppers take a monthly cut to let the business roll. They love me! Quick cash is everywhere.'

'Countdown,' I sang, still feeling as if in a dream. Then, I noticed the male nurse usher Lucy out; it seemed in slow motion.

'I'm going to catch up with the crew, to party. The Painters and Dockers are playing; we're all going out to the Bolt,' she said as the room began to spin, and spin and spin again. Lucy spotted a doctor who looked like had a brick to his ear. 'I'll catch ya later, bro.' She followed him as she left the room.

'Excuse me, what the hell is that?' she asked the doctor.

'A phone,' the man said and scurried away.

'What the hell?' a young, hyped-up girl said, quietly amused, while the sound of a penny dropped on the cold hospital tiles. 'Fucking new, it,' she squandered.

Conjured sadness had built up inside. Silence hung in the air as she walked away. She was misunderstood and was acting nervous. We had sacrificed a lot over the years. She was no longer a sweet little thing. Sometimes I got a little pissed off with her. She didn't do anything by halves. She'd lost control.

I felt lonely. With crazy eyes, I looked into my arm where I was injected. 'More, more, more morphine,' I sang, along with *Countdown* theme song. I was dizzy, then moments later, blanked out.

I woke up, coming to from my slumber.

A female nurse came over and checked on me, singing John Farnham's new song, 'The Voice'. 'Whoa, ohh, ohh, ohhho,' she continued humming away.

She was beautiful, checking my eyes, my pulse, and my head. While she inspected the stitches in my head, her breasts were close to my face. I smiled. She pulled away, screwed up her face, and said, 'Well, you're alive, all right.'

As she walked away, I asked her what her name was and told her she was beautiful. Ignoring this, she handed me my breakfast tray, turned on the TV, and left the room. The morning news was on. My breakfast was cold. I vaguely recalled what Lucy told me about the night, thinking, *Did we do it? Did we win?* I was trying to remember.

She mentioned INXS and *Countdown*. I was on morphine, but I was sure she'd said *Countdown*. I was powerless to shake the *Countdown* theme track out of my head. *Wait, what did she say about that?* I tried the best to gather my erratic thoughts. My head was aching. A blood clot that had built up grew; then it exploded in my brain.

I needed brain surgery to remove a bulge or ballooning in a blood vessel in the brain. The bulge often looked like a berry hanging on a stem.

A brain aneurysm can leak or rupture, causing bleeding into the brain, causing a hemorrhagic stroke. Most often, a ruptured brain aneurysm occurs in the space between the brain and the thin tissues covering it. This type of hemorrhagic stroke is called a subarachnoid hemorrhage.

A ruptured aneurysm quickly becomes life-threatening and requires prompt medical treatment, of which I received. It was a successful operation, and I was lucky to be alive. Banged up big time.

Slowly, while eating the horrendous hospital breakfast, the news was on the anchor, explaining how Lindy Chamberlian had been released, which caught my attention. I always thought she was innocent. Then they crossed over to a female reporter. It was the prim-and-proper woman who covered the story about the school shooting. It came on as breaking news. I gingerly sat up, my neck in a brace. Teenagers were caught up in a wild brawl outside the

Bolt nightclub. One had stab wounds, and two police officers were injured and taken to hospital.

A car crashed and blew up into a ball of flames. Two people injured, one dead.

I stopped eating and breathing for a moment. Firefighters and ambulances were on the scene. I thought I saw Leigh in the background running down the street. Lifting myself carefully up on the bed, I turned up the TV, listening closely to the reporter, word by word.

'We believe the incident is attached to a wild brawl outside the club. Reports are that the incident was between two bands, at the ending of the infamous Battle of the Bands event. Eyewitnesses say that a stolen vehicle was used as a getaway car, containing four youths.'

Then *boom*, Gazza and Daz were on TV being thrown in the back of the divvy van by three officers. I spotted the copper I had a fallout with.

'The identities of the people in the car are not yet known,' the reporter said.

My heart pounded.

'Although we believe the people are friends or acquaintances of the band.'

My heart stopped. Life stopped; it became slow motion.

Wait a minute. I'm still dreaming. Surely, that can't be Lucy, Tommy, or Melissa in that car, my brain cried. Becoming nauseated, I struggled to breathe.

Then instantaneously, a commotion broke out: a racket of people yelling, the sound of hurried footsteps coming up the passageway outside my ward. I looked out towards the doorway and caught a glimpse of two beds being wheeled down the passageway, with doctors, nurses, and police as escorts. Sure enough, my nightmare had become real; I noticed the second person was Gazza.

Brokenhearted, my thoughts turned toward my sister. *Is she alive? Is she dead?*

Faced with reality, in a world of pain, I was pinned to the bed, screaming for help and a nurse. Finally, one arrived. I frantically asked about the two guys and if they had seen my sister.

More yelling and screaming. My own.

Another male nurse arrived, telling me to calm down. He confirmed the identity of the two people. It was Gaz and Daz.

'Lucy! Lucy! LUCY!' I screamed, thrashing on the bed. Hysterical tears poured down my face.

The male nurse assured me there was no sign of Lucy, that one female died instantly at the scene. In shock, thoughts of Melissa raced through my mind.

He administrated another dose of morphine into my arm to calm me down. 'Lucy!' I yelled...until the pain and anguish went away.

Was Lucy in the sky while I'm still high? The song we made up all made sense now.

I was singing in my mind. It seemed like some impossible dream. Childhood memories flooded my mind and the places and faces we had seen together...childhood memories. Like a roll of the dice, she had sacrificed her love for me.

Spoilt little bitch, she had it all, defied all principles, life as well.

'Oh, Lucy... Oh, Lucy, no more. What the fuck is happening?' I mumbled to myself.

Clearly in a state of trauma, unaware of the injections of morphine I had been given moments ago, I lay in the hospital bed. Slipping in and out of consciousness, I had the sense of moving up or through a narrow passageway, having a spontaneous out-of-body experience. I never really believed in angels or demons or ghosts until now. Was I in a scary horror movie after this near-death experience? Visions of an angelic Lucy floating calmly upwards towards the sky encountering beings of light and a God-like vision of Mother's open arms made me shudder. Sweating, more thoughts of living on the farm, my grandparents in the car crash, the fire that went through our property and destroyed next door's property flashed through my mind.

All these sensations plus childhood memories and vivid emotions poured through my body and mind. I heard soft voices, nonphysical sounds. The news reader continued, 'Two young males and a female have been rushed to the Royal Melbourne Hospital with burns, and...' Her voice slowly faded as my eyelids started to close.

Completely aware of my surroundings yet feeling without control, I started going into a very relaxed, meditative state.

I experienced feelings of peace, no pain. The 'Mind Awake, Body Asleep', it was time to let go and feel free. It seemed like I was looking down upon myself lying helplessly in the hospital bed alone, frightened and scared. Only for a second, I wanted to change my mind, my spirit.

'No way, not today, I'm not dying alone like this.' Thoughts of the innocence, of a little a boy playing in the creek with his sister, childhood memories passed through. A clear vision of my mother's angelic face looked down from Heaven upon me. Like a stepping stone, they guided and lead the way. Feeling slightly foolish, even somewhat surprised, I denied the pain relentlessly, or was it a blessing?

'Fight. Fight for it, Archie; don't let your dream diminish now, chase your dream,' a beautiful, pure, calming voice spoke and appeared like a choir of angels from above. 'Be courageous,' the voice whispered. The look on her face shining through the clouds made my heart beat better.

The time is now. We had to make this happen. Time has told.

Astonishingly, a force-of-nature ghost-like figure thrust its way into my limp body. Gasping for air, my eyes widened like an owl in the dead of the night. That was the moment I was destined to find out what happened to my sister: dead or alive.

I never really believed in Heaven or Hell, angels, demons, or ghosts...until now. Had my soul been sold to rock 'n' roll or the devil?

Was this dream over? Had it just begun, or was it...The End?

Thoughts of the 2000-word advanced English assignment that Miss Cummins had given us about chasing our dreams scattered my brain. A surge of inspiration flowed like Niagara Falls. Picking up my notepad and pencil, I began to reflect, and words poured out of my soul. There was no stopping me now.

Would I do it all over again? Bloody oath, I would. I closed my eyes, cleared my head, and visualized for a minute or two. Then put pen to paper.

This was one lesson I thought I would have learnt my mistake. It was the start of a journey riddled of recklessness, booze, drugs, sex, crime, religion, but best of all, rock 'n' roll and good times.

It was 1982. A warm, clear autumn day.

The echo of white galahs squawked throughout the terrain. Their wings flapped wildly as our dog, Rusty's, barking spooked the birds. The birds flew to the nearby dry bull oak across our farm, nestling near the border of South Australia and Victoria.

The warm autumn breeze blew through Lucy's long blond hair. Wild sundried thistle along the property sang soulfully while the windmills worked harder than ever.

Mother was dead.

The End.

Melissa
TCJ
ARCHIE
Gaz & Daz
Mary & E

Leigh 87

The Gang 86
Tommy 87

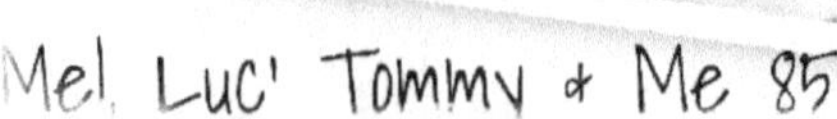

Mel, Luc' Tommy & Me 85

A story by Archie Saunders

This is one lesson I thought I would've learnt form my mistakes.
It was the start of a journey riddled with recklness, booze
rugs, sex, crime, religion, but best of all, rock 'n' roll and good times.
Its was It was a warm, clear autumn day in 1982.
The echo of white galahs squawked throughout the terrain.
Their wings flapped wildly as our dog, Rusty's, barking
spooked the birds. The birds flew to the nearby dry bull oak
cross our farm, nestling near the border of Sth Australia & Victoria..

he warm autumn breeze blew through Lucy's long blond hair..
Wild sundried thistle along the property sang soulfully.
While the windmills worked harder than ever.

MOTHER WAS DEAD.

Acknowledgments

Thank you to everyone who has endured listening to my performances over the decades, especially the band mates and friends who I have made music with, jamming with over the years.

I would particularly like to thank Katharine Sands from NYC who helped me with initial editing, collaboration, and motivation. Katharine's years of experience, especially her patience, is well and truly acknowledged. I did go on to write another 15,000 words, which I believe is called rewriting. I follow this by thanking the amazing Cynthia Hilston from Ohio, USA, who helped with the layout, formatting, and dialogue, keeping consistency about the storyline, which was urgently required. I also want to thank Nicole Hayes for her wisdom and experience over a two-day writing course, which made me realise I still had a lot of work to do. A huge thank you to Australian Self-Publishing Group and Surendra Gupta for their patience during the longevity with all my re writing and edits.

I must express my gratitude to my Rock and Rockstar, Rocking Robyn, for her valuable contributions and help with line edits while working in the corporate world, for devoting her time, implementing in this project, while giving me strength, passion, inspiration, and belief to finish and pursue the dream and vision to write this story when I clearly and nearly had given up. I also wish to express my gratitude to all her family and friends enduring what they had to go through and accepting me for who I am.

To 13-year-old Chamois, the puppy, little brave Chammy, three neck surgeries and three scares. My best friend. We cuddle, we play, we are inseparable; you make me feel normal again.

I would like to recognise the importance of the Nhill Aerodrome Base and acknowledge The Netherby Hotel, The Beatles, INXS, 3rs.org, and all the acts and labels made reference to. In particular, I wish to thank the acts and agents who gave me the permission to mention and have reference to them and be a part of this little story: Painters and Dockers, The Waterboys, Molly Meldrum, and *Countdown*.

The song 'Lucy's in the Sky and I'm Still High' was created in a house with mates Dave, Allan, Bous, Andy, and myself back in the early '90s. The song '4 Hours' was written and inspired by the Columbine High School shooting and is dedicated to all the families and victims on April 20, 1999.

Thank you to my older brothers and sister for being supportive over the years and the childhood memories we created growing up. Thank you to my parents, who gave us a terrific upbringing and values. To this day, my father is the best singer I have ever heard, and my caring, nurturing, beautiful, loving mother, whose traits and advice I cherish and honour, I am truly blessed that I have thankfully inherited.

To all my friends, you have become friends for a reason, friendships I do not take for granted.

Music makes people unite and happy.

Be kind to one another.

Enjoy life today.

Not tomorrow.